MW00627330

SisQo's Perfect Christmas

A SAUCER AND MOON COLLECTED EDITION

Written by

Tilesha Brown & SisQo

Cover & Insert Illustrations by

Savannah Alexandra & SisQo

Chapter Illustrations by

Eric Savage

SAUCEBERRIe moon | LOS ANGELES

Copyright © 2018 by Tilesha Brown.

All rights reserved. No part of this publication may be reproduced, distributed or transmitted in any form or by any means, including photocopying, recording, or other electronic or mechanical methods, without the prior written per-mission of the publisher, except in the case of brief quotations embodied in critical reviews and certain other noncommercial uses permitted by copyright law. For permission requests, write to the publisher, addressed "Attention: Permissions Coordinator," at the address below.

Tilesha Brown/SAUCEBERRIe MOON PUBLICATIONS, LLC

11657 Sitka Street El Monte, CA/91732

Publisher's Note: This is a work of fiction. Some names, characters, places, and incidents are a product of the author's imagination. Locales and public names are sometimes used for atmospheric purposes.

Los Angeles / Tilesha M. Brown — First Edition

Printed in the United States of America

Table of Contents

For my family, who has given me a collection of perfect Christmases and the invaluable gift of storytelling.

And for the Andrews, who support and inspire me daily.

-Tilesha

Dedicated to my family... I love you.

-SisQo

PROLOGUE

Twinkle, Twinkle QoQo Star

It all started with mooncakes… on a snowy Christmas night.
QoQo tried her hardest to get the sprinkles just right.
With her daddy gone and her mother asleep…
It was her job to make sure they were perfectly sweet.

See, QoQo had been planning this for a very long time,
She'd covered all her tracks and practiced every line.
She was just the baby, but tonight was the night…
That she'd become a star… the brightest of the bright.

She'd heard of Genie Moon only through the grapevine,
But she thought, "If she could grant my classmates' wishes, she could grant mine."
So it was off to the kitchen to prepare her favorite snack,
She'd practiced for days— mooncakes back to back.

First, she'd whip up the batter with care,
Then, whisper magic words into the night air.
She'd sit real tight for the sign that meant "yes."
And she'd smile to herself, knowing what was ahead.

QoQo's plan was quite brilliant, you see.
She had a plan to bring her father home on Christmas Eve.
He had the incredibly cool job of a rock star, she knew.
But having him gone on holidays was always so cruel.

So she wished and wished with all her might.
And to be sure, she'd practiced until it was right.
There was no way they'd open up their presents alone.
Not without daddy safe at home.

But that wasn't all, no- that was just the half…
She had one more wish… and it could turn out bad.
For, this one required great sacrifice.
And if things didn't go right, she'd pay with her life.

But to her, the reward was so worth the risk.
And if it worked out, it'd be her very last wish.
She'd worked it all out with Genie so far:
Tonight… she'd trade her dad's gift for her very own star.

If all went well, she'd become just like him
She'd travel the world, sing with her own flash spin.
But if it didn't go so well… then, all would be lost.
They'd fall from grace… and it'd be all her fault.

But she couldn't dwell on the bad, she had to believe.
With Genie Moon on her side, she could do anything.
So at 8 on the dot, as she saw a star fall,
She wished that by morning, she'd be the biggest star of them all.

1

All I Want for Christmas is Food!

Lightning never strikes the same spot twice... unless you were Kimiqo Andrews.

In her case... she found that six times was, in fact, the limit.

That's exactly how many times lightning struck the big house on Sweet Maple Drive on the days leading up to Christmas Day. Every morning, her mother would go out to the mailbox and find it burnt to a crisp where the lightning had hit it. She'd scratch her head in confusion and then call the city to repair it. By the sixth day, which happened to be Christmas Eve, her mother had screamed so loud that she thought the roof might blow, but QoQo (pronounced just like the warm drink) just sat quietly at the table eating her breakfast, smiling ever so slightly to herself. For this, she thought, was how she knew her most important wish would come true that very night. It was what people called "a sign." And she was ready for what would happen that night.

Or so she thought.

You see, that night, as the sweet smells of milky coconut and syrupy sugar drifted out of the kitchen, she tiptoed from one corner of the room to the other... carefully, carefully preparing the most special snack. Everyone had gone to sleep early, but every once in a while, the little girl they called QoQo raised her ear toward the stairs to make sure no one was awakened by the clouds of sweet and nutty smoke floating through the air. Each time she was sure that no one was up, she breathed in the magical scent of her grandmother's famous Vietnamese snow skin mooncakes with special coconut filling into her tiny little nostrils. Her soft waves were held up by pink rubber bands on either side of her round face, while her eyes seemed to fill with the creamy smells of the cakes she was making.

Now, it goes without saying... QoQo was no ordinary girl. In fact, her father had insisted on naming her "QoQo Star" after an actual star her mother had given him on his birthday before QoQo was born. And then by QoQo's second birthday, she'd sealed the deal by singing the letters of the alphabet in the perfect key. Unbeknownst to her, this was a test that SisQo had done with all three of his children. His first daughter, Shaione, had been able to sing the alphabet song in perfect pitch. Her brother Ryu was OK, QoQo guessed, but now she'd passed the test too! He officially declared her a star. That was a special day for QoQo because her father was also no ordinary man.

No, he was one of the biggest stars... a rock star, to be exact.

He traveled all over the world performing and making music for people who went crazy over his songs. Sometimes she even got to see him on TV. So if he said she was a star, she believed it.

The only problem was… he was always off doing star stuff, and she was always stuck at home with her brother Ryu, who was not a star by any means, in her opinion. She guessed he was OK. He could recite all of the planets by heart, and he did go to the big kids' school. But he wasn't special like her…not if you asked QoQo. And what had really made her mad… madder than she'd ever been before… was that last month, her dad had called Ryu up on stage at a show to perform with him in front of everyone.

Ryu got to do the super-cool-flash-spin with Dad and everything!

It just wasn't fair. If anyone was meant to be on that stage that night, it was supposed to be her. And for months, she'd plotted her revenge. She was going to take this star thing to a whole other level, and she didn't need help from her uncool big brother to do it. She was going to do it all on her own.

The only thing she needed was a mooncake… or ten!

And a footstool.

Well, she'd already found the footstool behind the couch and was pushing it into the kitchen when she decided to go back over the plan in her head one more time. See, it all started months ago when she'd overheard Betsy Carter talking on the playground at pre-K. At first, she thought she'd heard wrong. She was only three years old, but she knew that magic wasn't real.

Her mom had told her that it was nice to think and dream, but you had to always be smart and have your head on straight when it came to real life. Real life stuff was making sure you finished your homework and double checking that you looked both ways before crossing the street. Fairy godmothers weren't going to magically appear to help you do those things, her mom had said. You had to rely on your own self for real life stuff like that. So for QoQo, her dreams of magic stayed inside of her head or in the books she read at the library.

That was, until the first week of February. She'd heard Betsy talking to the other girls at school about Genie Moon… how if you had a wish, any wish, you could call on Genie to grant it. The only thing was that you had to know the magic words and you had to know the kind of payment Genie accepted. This made QoQo perk up. She'd heard her grandmother talk about Genie Moon once or twice, but she hadn't paid it much attention. But now that Betsy was talking about it… she thought long and hard. She had a wish, alright. It was a wish that she knew nothing but magic could make come true. What she didn't know was what the magic words were. And what kind of payment did the moon accept? Later that night, she looked up at the glowing ball of light and wondered... how could she figure this out?

Well, little did she know... the answers were about to drop into her lap...or if we're being honest... they dropped into her dinner.

Here's how it happened.

It was another night that her father was away. She knew he was working, but she wanted him home because it was about to be Chinese New Year and she wanted them all to celebrate together. But he was working, and that was that. She was sad, but she'd learned that if she was a big girl while he was away, they would play extra long when he got back.

It was a cold night, so pho (a very delicious Vietnamese soup) was on the menu. And tonight, they were ordering it in from a restaurant so, of course, with it came fortune cookies. This was QoQo's favorite part. No one could ever resist reading those little strips of paper that tell the future. And this was especially true for QoQo. She absolutely loved cracking open those fresh, buttery cookies and finding out what the universe had planned for her next.

But nothing could've prepared her for what this particular cookie said that day.

Now, since QoQo was only three years old, she couldn't read yet. She was still working on that, but her mother never minded reading her fortunes to her. And even Elizabeth was surprised by what seemed to not just be written, but *inscribed* onto the white piece of paper that was tucked inside of the small pastry.

"Your wishes will be granted at the second floor window on September 24th.
-G.M."

And that was it. It was the day her life changed. Of course, her mother hadn't understood. Elizabeth crumpled up the piece of paper and mumbled something about it being a mistake before throwing it away. But after dinner was over, after the dishes had been put away, and QoQo had been tucked into bed, she'd waited for the soft sound that meant her mother had closed her bedroom door. When she'd heard it, she sneaked down and got the gently crumbled piece of glossy paper out of the trashcan and looked at it one more time under the gleaming spotlight of the moon.

She knew what the words were now after hearing Elizabeth read them out loud. But even though her mother had thought nothing of it, QoQo knew that this was no mistake. This fortune was meant for her. And QoQo knew because September 24th was her birthday! And it was no coincidence that it had mentioned the second floor window. Her bedroom was on the second floor and she always, always stared out of her window when she made her wishes. She'd learned that from the movies. And she knew that this was a special note because she recognized the initials at the bottom. She happened to know her letters very well, thank you very much!

And "G.M." could only stand for one thing: Genie Moon.

And in fact, Genie had sent the note. In fact, she hadn't been able to resist. QoQo was one of her favorite little girls in the whole, wide universe. Even though they'd never officially met, she knew QoQo's grandmother, her mother, and her uncle. She'd watched over them for as long as she could remember and they were one of the highlights of Genie's career. See, Genie could see into the future and so her fascination with them was not only because of what they'd done up until now... but mostly because of what she knew they would eventually become.

And of course, Genie had known that QoQo would one day make a wish that would change their entire lives. The only thing Genie couldn't figure out was why her time hopper... the small clock she kept in her pocket to see the future with... just would not tell her what QoQo's wish would be. And this was quite odd. For the moon was very, very old and she couldn't remember ever, ever, ever having this problem.

She'd always been able to see everything! The future, the past, and even things people tried to hide from her in the present. This was a gift that had come from God himself, and so she was quite confused when it just stopped working all of a sudden. But she didn't let that stop her. She would just have to wait until QoQo actually made her wish to find out what it was, Genie supposed.

After all, she thought, *how crazy could it be?*

She would find out just a few months later.

Time slipped away from QoQo over the next few months. She kept the fortune underneath her pillow, but with play dates and school and the responsibilities of having to enjoy every last day of her summer break, it was September 1st before she remembered that she only had 23 days to figure out how this "wishing on the moon" thing really worked. Her friends at school wouldn't tell her exactly how to do it because they were mean girls and didn't think she was special enough to talk to Genie... even after she told them that she'd gotten the note in the fortune cookie.

"That's *not* how it works!" said Betsy on the playground the next day, "Genie's not Chinese!"

"I'm not Chinese either!" screamed QoQo, "And how do you know what Genie is?! I bet you don't even really know her!"

But by that time, Betsy had already walked across the playground to join the other popular pre-K girls. When Betsy reached them, they all pointed in QoQo's direction, laughing.

Tears welled up in her eyes as she turned her back on them all and went back into her classroom to think. She just had to figure this out somehow.

There had to be clues somewhere. Genie couldn't expect her to figure this all out on her own. She was only three! She needed to know what time to meet Genie. She needed to know the magic words. And she knew she needed payment. But what did Genie like? She had so many questions and no one to ask. The whole thing made her want to cry even more.

But what good would that do? Her mother had always taught her that when there's a problem, you do two things: think about all the things your mother taught you and figure out if you already know the answer… OR talk to an adult about it if you're in trouble and need help as soon as possible.

Well, she had a problem. And she needed an answer as soon as possible. So, she guessed she would have to talk to an adult.

QoQo pretty much knew for a fact that her mom had never spoken to the moon. And the clock was ticking, so she turned to the only other adult that she'd ever heard talk about Genie: her grandmother.

Now, she had to wait a few days to see her grandmother

because she wasn't allowed to use the telephone by herself just yet. And she didn't want anyone else listening to this question. No, she'd have to wait to talk to her grandma about this face-to-face.

It was a Thursday morning…only nine days before the big day… when she finally got her grandmother alone. To do it, she had acted like she was sick on the very day she knew her mother had an appointment. She knew that her mother would have no choice but to ask her grandmother to take care of her and that would be her chance to get all of the information she needed.

The only problem with this plan was that her brother Ryu was up to something that day, too.

He must've used his extra sensitive big brother sixth sense and figured out that this was super important to her, and now he wanted to ruin it. Or worse yet, what if he'd found her fortune? Suddenly, she really did feel sick. Her stomach felt like it was turning flips and she thought her breakfast might come up as she tried to think back to where she'd left it. She'd been careful, hadn't she?

Well, there was no way to be sure because they were already in the car on their way to grandma's by the time she thought about this. She looked at Ryu out of the corner of her eye. He was looking at his portable video game thingie so intently that he didn't even notice her staring. She was thinking about what he might look like or what he might say if he had, in fact, read her fortune.

After all, he'd told her once that he knew Genie Moon too. He'd said that they were close friends. And now, all of a sudden, he was saying that he felt a little sick too… ON THE SAME DAY as her important talk. And Mom had believed him because she thought it might've been something weird going on with dinner the night before. So she'd fed them both oatmeal to coat their tummies that morning and now, they were both headed to Grandma's house with two separate plans.

She could tell that he wasn't really sick. But ever since he'd gone and started hanging out with the big kids at school, she had no idea what he was thinking anymore. He never wanted to play outside with her, and he never let her play his stupid games. So she sat there wondering just what he was up to. But she didn't say a word. She wouldn't ask him a thing. She'd just have to be extra careful not to let him hear her conversation with Grandma.

That day, it had been tough getting Grandma all by herself. From the moment they got to her cinnamon-sweet smelling house, Ryu just wouldn't leave them alone. She thought he would surely want to play his game, or eat a snack, or go to bed since he was sooooo "sick". But no, when she sat next to Grandma on the couch to watch a movie, there was Ryu. When she went into the kitchen while Grandma fixed a pot of tea, there he was again. He wasn't saying much, but she got the impression that he was waiting for something.

But then, he seemed to give up right after lunch time. After scarfing down his peanut butter and jelly sandwich, he rubbed his belly and stretched out on the sofa with his game and zoned out onto another planet like he always did. And that's when QoQo knew. This was her chance. She had to act now.

Finally, she thought.

And when she followed the scent of her grandmother's cinnamon-coated apron, she ended up in the laundry room, where she found the four-foot-eleven woman smiling at her over a basket of freshly dried towels. QoQo just loved the scent of freshly washed clothes. It made her want to curl up in them and sleep forever. But right now, she had work to do. And she thought that this was the perfect place to ask her grandmother the questions that had been burning in her mind since she first opened the fortune cookie on Chinese New Year—nearly eight months ago!

"What is it, QoQo?" her grandmother asked.

And the little girl stepped forward, beckoning for the older woman to stoop to her level to hear a secret.

Her grandmother didn't hesitate before setting the towels on the dryer and bending down onto one knee. She pressed her ear to the girl's cupped hand and listened. In the moments that followed, QoQo told her grandmother all about Genie Moon and how she'd written to her on a fortune and how she needed to make a wish on her birthday that would be the biggest wish she ever dared to imagine. She whispered and whispered. And the old lady smiled and smiled.

Now, secrets between a grandmother and her grandchild are strictly confidential information— "confidential" means that no one can ever know the things they told each other when no one else was around. But you can bet that there were plans made that night— exciting plans that would change the entire rest of QoQo's life. Her grandmother knew that QoQo was special. She was smarter than any other almost-four-year-old she'd ever met... much smarter than even her parents or the girls at school knew. And she knew that if anyone could pull this plan off, it was her. She simply reminded her that if she had faith... the kind that never wavered... she could do anything she set her mind to.

Besides... QoQo's grandma had a little secret of her own... which we'll find out real soon.

But for now, that brings us back to Christmas Eve... when the entire plan that they came up with in that laundry room was about to go down.

The thick scent of Christmas hung in the air like

ornaments on a tree. It instantly gave you the feeling of the holiday settling in. In the next room, the sweet smells made QoQo's mother, Elizabeth, sink deeper into her blankets, her dreams of dancing sugar plums getting tastier by the minute. The warmth of the fireplace followed QoQo through the house, past the Christmas tree, and down the basement stairs as she grasped her teddy bear tight for protection.

This was such an important night, and she could feel her heart rattling against her little chest as she went. Even though this was the moment she'd been waiting for… the moment she'd prepared for since September… the moment that would change her entire life… she was still nervous. And not just a little bit.

This was the kind of nervous that made your stomach turn in knots, the kind that gave you butterflies in your throat… this was the kind of nervousness that made you…

CLAP, POP, BOOM!

The noise broke her nervous train of thought.

What was that?

That was her first thought. But the thoughts after that came as a series of questions: Had her mother woken up? Was her brother up to something that might ruin everything she had planned? For a quick moment, she actually felt a wave of panic… but then… all she felt was relief. Maybe someone was about to ruin everything. Then, she wouldn't have to do this thing… this crazy, scary thing that she couldn't make up her mind about. Wouldn't that be a relief?

But no.

It only took a few seconds for her to figure out that it was neither her mother nor her brother that had made the noise. And her father was away again, so it couldn't be him. In fact, she should have recognized the sound. It was the secret code that she and Genie Moon had worked out weeks ago.

"First, there'll be a clap of thunder," Genie had said, "Then a pop like a firecracker, and a boom like you've never heard it. That's when you'll know it's time."

QoQo now remembered clearly… Genie had taught her that the time between the first clap of thunder and the first flash of lightning told you exactly how far away a storm was. That was actually really cool information. If Genie stuck around, maybe QoQo would get good at science, after all. But there was no time for her to think of the future because right now, she knew she only had 45 seconds to get to the basement and in front of the marked spot to catch this particular flash. She and Genie had timed it precisely in their rehearsals since her birthday.

Genie would visit her and they'd go over and over it... and each time, QoQo would bring her grandmother's famous Vietnamese snow skin mooncakes, which she'd found out from grandma was Genie's favorite form of "payment". They'd rehearsed so much that QoQo could probably do this in her sleep. So why was she nervous? She decided that it was silly to be afraid.

So, QoQo gathered her courage and flew down the remaining ten steps, dashed across the cold, hard concrete floor to the middle of the basement. And when she was positioned just so, she shed her blanket and approached the old rickety boombox her grandmother had given her the last time she was at her house. One last plate of mooncakes in one hand and a fistful of the stardust Genie had given her in the other, she said the words:

"Dear Genie Moon, glowing and bright.
I wish upon you, this still starry night.
I... need my daddy home with the next flash of light."

QoQo let the next words fly out of her mouth in a very determined whisper just moments before the lightning actually flashed.

"Answer me swift, answer me sweet.
And please, Genie Moon, give me what I need."

With a blinding jolt, a bright, white light flooded the room, lighting the tiny girl from head to toe before traveling from her body to the small radio just before her. And in the next few minutes, she couldn't believe her eyes.

As QoQo bit down hard on her lip, she managed to open

her eyes slowly, slowly, slowly, until… she found herself face to face with her wish. Right there in the basement, beneath the glowing, hot fog of the moon, stood her father still completely shaken from what had just happened. It looked like a lightning bolt had just left a scar right down the middle of his face and right beside him, there were two other men whom she instantly recognized as Juice and Danni Boy... her father's backup dancers.

With the help of Genie Moon, she'd wished them right through the radio.

And even though they didn't know it yet, they were about to make every one of her dreams come true.

2

The Gift That Keeps On Spilling...

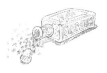

"Is this…?" SisQo's face said it all.

He was more confused than he'd ever been in his entire life.

"Wait a minute… weren't we just on stage in…?" asked Danni.

"Ummm…. somethin' tells me… we ain't in Dubai anymore, Toto," said Juice.

And then they spotted her. QoQo was standing in the corner of the room, holding her plate of mooncakes and staring at them wide-eyed, shocked, and trembling. She knew what she'd asked for. She'd practiced it a kajillion times. She knew what was supposed to happen. But this was magic on a whole other level. She'd never seen anything like this in her whole entire four-year life.

She'd just pulled her father and his dancers through the radio… back to her home… in the middle of their performance…

in Dubai!

For some reason, the room felt like it was spinning all around her. And the worst feeling came over her. For some reason, she suddenly felt ashamed. On top of that, she was confused and she didn't know what to do next. If you've ever felt all of those emotions hit you in one wave at the same time, you know exactly how much of a stomach ache it can give you, right?

You could hear the rumble in her tummy as she tried so hard to think of the right thing to say. But after a few seconds, she decided that she had to explain something. And so...very, very slowly, she poked one of her onesie covered feet into the one stream of light that was coming from the light bulb overhead.

"I can explain," she started when she was standing directly in the glow of the light.

"Well, someone had better!"

QoQo jumped and whirled around because the words hadn't come from her father standing right in front of her.

When she squinted her eyes and peered through the darkness and up the staircase, she saw her mother. Her eyes were filled with rage and her face as red as the garland on the Christmas tree. All QoQo could think was that she'd never been in this much trouble in her entire life.

"What... did... you do?!"

Her father's voice sounded like ice, immediately chilling her to the bone. Her teeth started to chatter so hard that after just seconds, they felt like they would shatter inside her mouth. As her mind raced, searching for the right words to explain, she was interrupted again.

"Ummm," she said, her eyes pointed to the ground.

Confusion and panic were written all over SisQo's face. You could see his brain frantically working to figure out how he'd gotten to the spot he was standing on. Was he dreaming? Was this a joke? It honestly felt like an episode of that show with Ashton Kutcher where they came out and told you that you'd just been Punk'd because, honestly... this didn't make any sense. But one look at his terrified daughter, standing in front of him, made him stop.

"QoQo, you won't get in trouble," he tried to sound calmer. "Just tell us what you did. How— what—"

Her father sounded afraid. The problem was that QoQo was afraid, too. It had all seemed so natural and reasonable to her when Genie was explaining it. But then again, when you're actually talking to the moon, anything seems possible, doesn't it?

Until you have to explain it to your parents, she thought. *That's when things get tricky.*

She opened her mouth, but nothing came out. And she did that three more times before thankfully, she saw her father's face soften. The confusion was still there. And for that, she couldn't blame him, but at least the anger was disappearing. He looked her in the eye for exactly ten seconds before holding out his arms for her to run into them. And that was all she needed.

The tears that had been waiting patiently behind her eyelids now flooded out and onto her cheeks, spilling onto her father's shirt as soon as she'd leapt into his embrace. She was sobbing uncontrollably when she felt his voice rumble beneath her body. She didn't know what he was saying at first, but when she opened her eyes and listened more closely, she did know that she felt better about explaining now.

"We need to know how this happened," she heard him say, "QoQo, how did we get through the radio?"

He didn't pull her away from his shoulders. He simply spoke into her ear and waited for her to answer. And she was glad. She preferred it that way. For, what she was about to say was about to sound so absurd, so outrageous… that she'd rather not see his reaction when she did tell him everything.

"It was Genie," QoQo mumbled, "Genie and me."

She felt her father's arms go still around her. She knew she still had explaining to do, but she didn't want to face them… not yet, anyway. So she clung to her father's neck and spoke into his shirt. She knew that they could probably barely hear her, but this was the only way she felt comfortable.

But before she could finish her explanation, there was another voice coming from the top of the staircase. And this time, it actually brought QoQo some relief.

"Genie talked to *you*?" the voice asked, very curiously.

And in a matter of a split second, the entire room looked up to face Ryu, who actually sounded excited and just a tad bit jealous that this was all happening. And this was unusual. Nothing about QoQo excited him… ever. But it was obvious from the pitch of his voice that this was different. Something about QoQo mentioning Genie Moon had stirred something in him. He felt some kind of way about Genie speaking to her. But why? Over the summer, he'd told her that he and Genie were friends. He'd bragged about all of the adventures he'd been on with her. Every time he went to their grandparents' house alone, he'd come back home with brand new stories about having all his dreams come true all because he knew how to talk to the moon.

But what she didn't know was that Genie Moon had never actually spoken to Ryu. Those stories he'd told her were just that... stories. No matter how hard he tried, no matter how many times he called on her... and said the words... Genie had never answered him back. Telling QoQo that he and Genie were friends was just his way of getting back at her for little things like borrowing his toys and annoying him and his friends on the playground.

QoQo was the baby and she always got her way, no matter what. So he told her tall tales to make her jealous, because everyone knew that jealousy was the best punishment... especially when it came to baby sisters. So, he would go on and on about how she missed out on the adventures he had with Genie, and she never knew if the things he told her were real or not... until she'd gotten her own message that night inside the cookie.

"You know about this... this Genie Moon, too?" SisQo asked his son.

Ryu was still looking at QoQo, his eyes the size of silver dollars. Disbelief made him zone out for a couple of seconds, but his mother didn't have the patience for this at all.

"Ryu, tell us right now what your sister is talking about," she snapped. "What is going on?"

Ryu looked up at her all of a sudden, like he'd been snapped out of a trance. He couldn't speak... or move, it seemed. And just when SisQo and Elizabeth were starting to get really frustrated, QoQo spoke up again.

"I think we can show you better than we can tell you," she said softly.

The words came out like a whisper, but the room was so silent, you could hear a pin drop, so everyone heard her well enough... and soon, they were all marching up the basement stairs together.

"Where are we going, QoQo?" Elizabeth finally spoke.

QoQo was now leading the entire family, plus Danni and Juice, up the stairs in the house now. But still, no one had said a word about what was actually going on. Elizabeth was starting to get a little freaked out by all of this and it was making her a little angry.

"Are we not the parents here?" She rounded on SisQo. "Why are the kids in control right now?"

"Because we already done came through a radio, woman!" he hissed under his breath so that only she could hear., "A radio, Elizabeth! Who knows what else they can do! I don't know what your plan is, but I'm followin' the little one!"

SisQo had started to think that just maybe his kids had powers beyond his understanding. Flashes of Harry Potter, Family Guy, and the kids in Disney movies started to swim inside his mind.

This was some really freaky stuff, he thought to himself.

The last thing he wanted to do was upset the one that just pulled him thousands of miles through a radio. That was some magic he was not equipped to battle with at the moment. Actually, he never wanted to fight with that kind of magic... ever. His mind was buzzing with all kinds of thoughts like this as QoQo led them all into her room with giant dollhouses and stuffed toys all neatly stacked in every corner.

The entire room was a lot more inviting than the basement. The cool blues and purples covering the walls were calming as the moonlight poured in, making the colors bounce around the room. It made them all a little more comfortable with all of the tensions flying. But after they'd let out a deep breath or two, all of their eyes shifted back to the elephant in the room... the baby elephant... AKA QoQo.

"Ok, so..." she said, twisting her fingers around her hair, "It all started when I got a fortune cookie in my Chinese New Year dinner."

Everyone had questions in their eyes. You could practically hear their thoughts. *Fortune cookie? Chinese New Year?*

"What does dinner have to do with how you pulled us through the radio?" Danni asked.

And he was leaning forward, waiting for the answer like his life depended on the information. By now, they were all so curious, so positively confused, and more than a little intrigued at the whole thing. They just wanted to understand. It was like magic... real life magic... and they needed to know the trick behind it all.

"Just let her finish," SisQo said, bending down to meet QoQo at eye level, "Go on."

And she did.

She told them all about the fortune, what it said, and how she'd prepared for months and months for this very day. She told them how Grandma had taught her how to make mooncakes to offer as payment, how Genie accepted her wish, then practiced and practiced for three whole months for the very moment that it would come true. She talked and talked, nearly running out of breath before she arrived at the end of the story.

"And that's when the thunder clapped, and the lightning struck... and BOOM... you came through the radio, Daddy!"

She was so emotional by the time she ended the story that she burst out in tears from the intensity of it all. This was the most she'd ever felt at one time and everything was bubbling up inside of her. She didn't even want to look at her father. She just knew that she was going to get in trouble. She'd broken about a bazillion rules— even rules that her parents hadn't even thought of. She'd done something dangerous and she hadn't thought about how she would explain it.

Now… she had no clue what was about to happen.

Elizabeth locked eyes with SisQo. This was the most ridiculous thing that had ever happened to the Andrews' family. And remember, they didn't lead an ordinary life. They were used to jet-setting all around the world, talking to all sorts of people about their beliefs, their wishes, and their dreams. But this…

"Nothing about this night makes any kind of sense," SisQo said after a few seconds.

"You're tellin' me," said Juice.

But Ryu had other ideas.

"Actually," he almost sang the words, "it all makes PERFECT sense!"

They all turned to look at him then. He hadn't spoken since they came up from the basement, but the looks on everyone's faces said that they were remembering how he'd somehow known what QoQo was talking about when the three guys had seemingly transported through the boombox. Whatever was going on, they were eager to wrap their heads around it… so they gave him their full attention.

"Weren't you listening?" Ryu nearly screamed.

They looked at each other one more time and then turned

back to Ryu.

"Listening to what? That whole make-believe story? Do you know what's going on with your sister?"

"It's not make-believe. Listen, Grandma told us the story… the story about Genie Moon."

"Genie who?" asked Elizabeth.

"The moon?" asked Danni. "She's talking about the MOON MOON? Like the actual moon in the sky?"

"Genie Moon!" Ryu was shouting now as he bounced on his heels with excitement. "The moon has a name. And if you know how to talk to her and what kind of payment she accepts, she grants all of your wishes!"

Just a tiny bit of recognition flashed across Elizabeth's face as Ryu spoke. Now that he mentioned it, she did remember how her mother would go on and on about the moon and how Genie, as she called her, actually listened. She would tell her and her brother Chris that Genie watched them… that she was the one that reported back to Santa whether they were naughty or nice. And if they were naughty, Elizabeth remembered, they'd get no presents on Christmas or money on Chinese New Year, which was always just a couple of months later.

But of course, she didn't believe in such things. And as far as she was concerned, neither did her brother. There was absolutely no way they were passing that kind of fantasy down to their children. It didn't seem natural. It never occurred to Elizabeth that her mother would tell her kids about it even if she didn't. Just the thought made her blush with embarrassment.

"Oh, honey… the moon can't—"

But she was cut off by a strange sound. Bells, then a kind

of... *twinkle*? Could you hear a twinkle? Elizabeth thought about this a moment, but then a second later, the sound came again, and this time, she was certain... there was no other word for it. You could most definitely hear a twinkle. But the next thought that Elizabeth was about to think got lost like some thoughts sometimes do when something extraordinary happens.

And this... was extraordinary.

At the very moment that SisQo and Elizabeth were about to ask themselves where the twinkling sound might be coming from, she saw his jaw drop. And a strange light was covering his face now. His eyes were big, and his skin was going pale. She could tell right away something was wrong.

"What is it?" she asked.

But he couldn't find his words. All he could do... was point.

Elizabeth whirled around on the spot where she stood, and when she did, her heart nearly thumped out of her chest. Right before them, held up by some sort of star-made magic, was the beautiful full moon that had been hanging in the night sky far, far away just moments before. And peering into QoQo's window where the entire Andrews' family (plus Danni and Juice) stood, were two eyes and a perfectly lipsticked pair of lips belonging to the most beautiful face they'd ever seen in their lives.

"Wha-?" mumbled Elizabeth.

"Who?" asked Danni.

"Told ya!" giggled QoQo, "Genie's here to help us get to the second part of my wish!"

"The second part of wha—?" SisQo said louder than he

meant to, "QoQo, I don't know what's going on, but—"

"Now, everyone settle down," Genie interrupted.

Everyone except QoQo and Ryu jumped at the sound of her voice. Shock pasted itself on their faces as she spoke each word. Her eyes sparkled and her nose did a little twist. She was in rare form tonight. For, Christmas was her favorite season, and this Christmas was turning out to be the best she'd ever had. Something special was happening tonight, and she could feel it in her lunar bones. They were tingling in ways they hadn't in a very long time. There was something about QoQo... something about her wishes... that excited Genie. And excitement was what she lived for!

"Now, I know this must be a great shock for you all and you're wondering what's going on," she said gently, "Well, what's going on is that your daughter made two wishes. But you already knew that. And you also already know what the first wish was... for her father to be home on Christmas Eve. But what you don't know is the second. That's why I'm here... and you might want to sit down for this."

By now, SisQo had seen more than his fair share of weird for the night, so no one had to tell him twice. He was moving across the room to QoQo's bed and starting to sit down before anyone could even blink. But he never took his eyes off Genie. He'd never seen anything quite like this. Her glowing face filled the window frame... and those eyes! He felt like they could really see through you to the inside.

And of course, he was right.

At that very moment, Genie could read his every thought.

Disbelief seemed to be the biggest thing floating through his brain at the moment, but there was also intrigue. She could tell that he was appreciating her for all that she was and that really made her happy. But she also knew that what she was about to tell him was going to be hard to hear. QoQo's wish was the biggest one she'd received in a very long time. What she was asking went against the laws of Lunar Magic and to make it happen, it would require great sacrifice.

And that's why she'd needed to be here... to present SisQo with a choice. And it wouldn't be an easy one.

"Ahem," she heard SisQo utter, "Ms., um, Moon?"

She almost laughed at this. No one had ever called her that before. All the kids knew to call her Genie. But these were special circumstances. She honestly couldn't remember the last time she'd been in the presence of so many adults. But this is how QoQo had dreamed it. And so, here they were.

"Yes, um, Mr. SisQo," she said jokingly. "What is it?"

"Is this a...?" He started. "Are you... real?"

Genie chuckled again. How many times had she heard this question? And she never got used to it. What was she really supposed to say, she almost wondered. It was so odd to her that humans would rather believe that there was just a big spotlight superglued to the heavens than to believe in anything bigger than themselves. Especially stars like SisQo, she thought, even though she knew that there was indeed something special about him. She knew that he did believe in something; she knew that he had seen magic happen before and that he left a little space in his heart for it always. But even still... he had to ask her this question like everyone else.

"I am," Genie decided to answer simply. "I am real."

She thought she saw him pinch himself several times very quickly and she guessed it was his way of making absolutely sure that he was awake. And in the next moment, he sat up straight and she knew he was ready to listen to whatever she had to say. And so Genie braced herself, because what she had to tell him was not easy or pleasant. It was uncomfortable even for her to ask… and she feared that it would make the night a lot harder for them all to get through.

"Lay it on me," he said simply, stealing a sideways glance at QoQo, "I'm ready."

He rubbed the top side of his jeans with the palms of his hands in anticipation.

"Well, QoQo has made a very important wish," she said slowly. "And if it's going to come true… there's something you'll have to give up."

SisQo stared at Genie blankly, waiting for her to finish.

There was a long pause. Elizabeth was nearly holding her breath, trying not to make a sound. Danni and Juice were backed up against the wall, ready to make a run for it as soon as SisQo said the word. But he seemed to be ready to take on this… spirit… or whatever she was. He was sitting closer to the edge of the bed now, looking her right in her eyes and trying hard to make sense of everything that was going on.

"SisQo, your daughter's wish is to become a star… like you," Genie spoke again, "She wants to be a singer and her wish… is to go to Hollywood to perform on stage this Christmas Eve."

Everyone was still. Nothing moved except the red that covered QoQo's face in embarrassment. She had never heard anyone else say it out loud and now she was afraid that they'd all laugh at her for making this kind of wish and interrupting Christmas with her crazy dreams.

But then something happened that changed everything.

Genie didn't say anything else, but it was what she did next that made everyone gasp.

She looked in the direction of a star hovering beside her and moved it toward the window using just her eyes. It floated like glitter in a snow globe until it was right in front of them all, leaving a trail of light behind it as it went. And when it was floating right in the window sill, just close enough for them to see, it burst into what looked like glittery flames. A great shout from everyone in the room rang out and they all jumped back, bracing for whatever was coming next. But nothing did, except in the space where they had just seen Genie's face appear in the window, there was now another view. It looked like the glass from a television set was floating mid-air, only nothing was showing now but the mirror image of SisQo in its reflection.

SisQo waved his hand to see if this mirror image would wave back.

It did.

"Hey, what's—"

But Genie's voice boomed over SisQo's again.

"Just… watch," she said, her voice echoing from behind the screen they were all watching.

Lo and behold, there he was. A tiny SisQo sitting at his desk in his bedroom, drawing sketches. His fingers were gripped around the pencil so intensely, and his eyes so focused that it seemed like he was in an entirely different dimension. Recognition flashed across the real SisQo's face. He'd forgotten just how much he used to draw as a child and how much that dream still meant to him. Tiny fireworks of excitement started to light up in his belly all of a sudden at the thought of starting to sketch again. In fact, he wished he could draw the moon he'd just seen up close and personal. He wondered if he could actually capture her essence after all these years of being out of practice.

But he didn't have too much time to dwell on that one memory because as quickly as it had come, it was gone again. And in its place came another one just as fast. This time, there he was with three other boys, practicing a dance move over and over in the middle of what looked like a tiny living room. Music, he thought. The dream that had actually come true.

He'd loved music for as long as he could remember. Nothing but his love for his family even came close to the love he had for the melodies he brought to life for a living. He stared as the younger vision of himself danced and opened his mouth to sing notes along with his brothers. He was lucky enough to still be doing that very thing over 20 years later, and he never felt as much gratitude as he did right at that moment.

He knew that what he did touched lives all over the world, but until one actually looks back at how far they've come, they never feel the full miracle of it all.

"Wow," was all he could say before the next memory came into focus.

This time, he was on television. Again, he was with his brothers on stage, doing their signature dance move and singing into fancy silver microphones to a crowd that was just as excited as they were. But that wasn't the point of this memory, SisQo slowly started to realize. It wasn't the stage that was the center of this vision. In fact, this wasn't about him at all.

At the bottom of the silver screen that this whole thing was playing out on, there was a slight bit of movement that caught SisQo's eye. And the more he stared, the more it moved into view. He stared and stared until understanding flooded his entire body. And then came the voice. It was low and still, but he already knew what Genie was going to say.

"Do you see your daughter?"

SisQo nodded.

No, this wasn't about him. This wasn't about the performance or the fact that he was on television. This was about his daughter and how she watched him. This was about how she studied him— admired him. And in the still quiet of the night closing in around them all, he could see her lips moving and hear a faint voice coming from her lips.

"Is she…?" he asked, swinging around to face QoQo with questions in his eyes.

"She is…" Genie answered for QoQo, "and she has a beautiful voice."

The real QoQo was now backed into a corner, her face red and her lips sealed tight. SisQo glanced at her quickly before turning back to Genie.

"Well… umm… if she wants to sing, then she can sing," he stated matter-of-factly. "… so what do we do? Are you going to grant her wish or…?"

"That's entirely up to you," Genie said again in a simple tone.

"How?" SisQo asked.

Frankly, he was tired of all of this mystery. Why couldn't she just answer a question with a straight answer? Why did he have to pull teeth to figure out why she was there and what they had to do to help QoQo?

"SisQo, you know just as well as anyone how the universe works. It only trades success for hard work," she said, "And since QoQo has not had the chance to actually work toward her dream... she's informed me that you've only been allowing Ryu to perform with you thus far."

SisQo looked back at QoQo.

"You could've... if you wanted.... why didn't you tell me?"

The last question came out in an exasperated tone, and he hung his head low. He couldn't deny it. He had let Ryu perform with him, but if he'd known that it was QoQo's dream, he would've....

"Nevermind the coulda, shoulda, wouldas," Genie interrupted his thoughts. "I've looked through the Lunar Laws of magic over and over, and it seems that she only has one other option... and that's where you come in."

SisQo couldn't stop himself from shivering at her words. He knew something was coming. He knew it was going to drop like a bomb. Genie had already said that this would require some sort of sacrifice. But what could it be? What could she take from him that would make QoQo a star overnight? He couldn't even—

Unless...

The thought struck him all at once like a bolt of lightning. His eyes widened as the last floating memory disappeared behind the cloud that it had come from. Suddenly, he knew what he would have to sacrifice. He knew what he had to do for his baby girl.

"My talent," he said softly. "I have to give it up so that she can have this wish."

Genie's eyes told him that he had guessed right. And when he looked more closely at Genie, he saw that she understood what he felt. She knew that this was the biggest sacrifice he'd ever faced. Dreams were often very hard to give up once they'd settled into the grooves of your heart. It was just like anything that belonged to you that was taken away. It was never easy.

Sometimes Genie wished that she had the simple tasks of her co-workers... her fellow wish-makers like the Tooth Fairy, Peter Rabbit, or even Jack Frost. They never had to make tough decisions like this one. They brought nothing but happiness while she was forced to teach hard lessons. Of course, that was why she and the others had never been close friends.... their differences made them keep their distance. It really was quite sad.

"It would be just for the night," Genie's voice traveled from the window like warm milk, and it soothed them all to hear this one bit of good news. "And the transfer will not harm you. Luckily, QoQo already has talent of her own. She doesn't need to take on yours. We simply need to hold it as payment in order to make her a true star quickly. It's the promise that does the trick."

SisQo nodded that he understood. But he also knew that there was something else... something else she hadn't said yet. And Genie knew that she couldn't make the transaction before telling the complete truth.

"Your schedule has changed, and you're now booked for the biggest show in Hollywood... tonight," she said. "But I must warn you...there is one catch. If, for whatever reason, QoQo should not complete this mission...if she does not make it to Hollywood to make her debut at precisely midnight, your talent will not be returned to you. For this works as all sacrifices do— there is much risk involved."

"Noooo!"

The voice came from the corner of the room that had been completely silent since Genie had arrived. Elizabeth's face appeared out of the shadows and tears were running down her face. She looked from QoQo to SisQo to Genie. Disbelief was in her eyes, and she was shaking from head to toe.

"Honey"—SisQo started to walk toward her.

"No, I can't let this happen. QoQo will grow into her talent. I'll get her singing lessons. I'll"—

But SisQo shook his head.

"No," he said softly, "Look at our baby. I didn't see it before, but I see it now. Look at her eyes… she's a dreamer. And I know what that feels like… to want someone to believe in you. You want someone to just wrap their arms around you and say that they know you have what it takes. If we don't do that for her now, with the moon as our witness… what message are we sending?"

And of course, Elizabeth knew he was right. But she didn't want any of them to face danger. She didn't want to risk anything when it came to any one of her kids or her husband. She just wanted to go back to bed and have this just be a bad dream that they laughed about in the morning.

But this wasn't a dream, and there was no turning back or waking up. She knew that when her husband made up his mind, there was no point in protesting. It was time to fold. And so she did. She nodded and then collapsed into SisQo's arms.

"We're going to Hollywood!" SisQo yelled out, then kissed Elizabeth's hair.

His excitement warmed them up, and they gave a little cheer when he said this. Even Genie chuckled a bit as a tear sneaked into the corners of her eyes.

There really wasn't anything like magic, she thought to herself, *Absolutely nothing.*

"But yo— it's already 9 o'clock! How are we gonna get all the way to L.A. by midnight?" Danni asked.

Everybody shot a questioning look at Genie.

"What, you got a sleigh or somethin'?" asked Juice.

"Well, as a matter of fact, I do!" Genie shouted.

And she pulled out a small bottle of what looked like fairy dust and handed it to QoQo.

"Thank you," the little girl said shakily.

"You know what to do!" Genie smiled.

And when QoQo looked up to meet her eyes, she caught Genie's wink. And all of a sudden… she did know! She knew exactly what to do. And nothing was going to stop her from taking charge of this night.

Move out of my way, she thought, QoQo Star is comin' to town!

A few seconds later, QoQo was shaking the small bottle of dust. Somehow she knew that with this magical powder, she could do anything. After all, she was a star herself now. Well, almost... and now she could have whatever she wanted at the snap of her very tiny fingers.

Soooo she poured a small pool of the glistening sand into

her left hand and dipped her right thumb and index into it. Then...

SNAP!

Her small, dust-covered fingers snapped together, and in the next second, there was a tiny cell phone in her palm... the very cell phone that her mother had told her she couldn't have for her birthday. Well, tonight, it was all hers. And right then, she had a very important call to make.

She focused on the phone where the secret app had appeared moments before.

Somehow she'd known just how to make it work and the words "OOBER JET" had appeared on the screen in large neon colors. And after she plugged in the secret code that just seemed to pop into her head at that very moment, that was it. She was in. Butterflies clapped wildly inside of her stomach. She'd waited SO long for this very moment.

"QoQo, what are you doing?"

When the order screen came up, it became even more real. She simply pushed the button and the next message on the screen told her that there was a sleigh making its way to their current location in 3 minutes.

"Calling our... car," QoQo told her mother.

She didn't want to really explain how magic transportation worked just yet. She knew her mother still didn't believe in all of this stuff. She may even believe that she was still dreaming, so she decided that she'd rather just show her mom than tell her anything more just yet.

"QoQo, I"— Elizabeth stopped herself from saying anything that might dash her daughter's dreams like SisQo had said, "Won't you let me help you, at least, honey."

But the little girl saw the doubt in her mom's eyes, and so she was determined to get this done on her own. She knew what Genie had promised her even if no one else believed her. And she had to prove this to them. It was important. She was sick of being treated like a baby. Tonight was the night that she let everyone know that she was a big girl, and that her dreams mattered too. Adults weren't always the ones that knew the most. There were some things that kids understood better than adults, she decided. And she was going to show them all.

All of a sudden, the screen lit up before her eyes. The numbers flashed in neon green saying that the next available sleigh would be there within minutes. All of a sudden, she couldn't help herself... she jumped so high into the air that she nearly fell out of the window right beside her.

"It's coming! It's coming!"

And within seconds, she peeked out of the window and saw the wheat-colored open sleigh racing across the sky above.

"QoQo, where...?" her mother started to ask.

But just as the words escaped Elizabeth's lips, they heard a sound on the roof. There was a boom and then... a jingle... and then... as they stood still, their eyes on the ceiling, they heard what they thought had to be a prank on their ears.

"Was that...?" SisQo started to ask.

"It's our ride!" screamed Ryu.

And it was just as if the mere thought brought them all out onto the roof by magic. Suddenly, they were all there. SisQo, Elizabeth, Ryu, QoQo, Juice, and Danni were all crowded around the sleigh, watching it glide to a complete stop right in front of them.

"Wow!" QoQo's frosty voice came out in billows of frozen air. "OOBER Sleigh!"

"Sleigh?" Elizabeth whispered.

And as soon as she said it, the step on its side was releasing and mechanically gliding down so that they could step into the sleigh safely. There was no driver... and there were no reindeer. The sleigh simply seemed to be alive. It was like a scene straight out of a kids' movie. And as the jingles died down, the wind blew fiercely, sweeping them off their feet and into the sleigh as if the vehicle was too impatient to wait for its passengers to snap out of their shock.

But all of a sudden, one more thud told them that this was all getting way too real for at least one of them.

They all turned to Elizabeth just as her body was going limp and she was slumping over in the sleigh. Her eyes were shut, and her breath had almost stopped. All SisQo could do was wrap his arms around her and try to bring her back to consciousness.

"This is gonna be a looooong night."

"Next stop... HOLLYWOOD!" Ryu shouted and nearly flew out of the sleigh from his excitement.

"Ryu, please sit down!" SisQo ordered, catching him before he flew away into the night sky.

Juice and Danni rode in two glass seats made especially for them in front of the sleigh, but when they looked back, they had to smile too. This was pretty amazing. There was never a dull moment with SisQo, but they had to admit that QoQo had beat him tonight. They'd never been on an adventure quite like this one. But Juice did wish they could get there faster!

"Who ordered OOBER POOL? It's gonna take us forever to get there!"

With that, they were off into the night sky, with only a twinkle of dust as their guide.

And no one noticed that the tiny bottle of stardust that QoQo thought was safe inside of her pocket was now turned over and the tiny specks of magic were now spilling out into the night air as they went.

3

Tingles All the Way...

By the time they reached 10,000 feet, everyone had just decided to go along with this plan that QoQo had cooked up. Did they all think it was absolutely crazy? Of course, but when the moon talks to you, what can you do but just shut up and go along with it? Besides, for the first time in a long time, there was a smile on QoQo's face.

SisQo knew that she'd been a little sad these last couple of weeks, but he could never figure out why. Now that he knew being away from home had caused his family so much stress, he was happy to be away from the stage and spending this very special night with them. There honestly was nowhere he'd rather be.

As for his voice, he'd have to worry about that later. He and QoQo would think of something before morning. Now that he saw what his baby girl was really made of, he was sure they could make it happen together. She'd done more than him in her little lifetime. He hadn't ever managed to talk to the moon. He smiled as she turned up the volume on the sleigh's radio system and sang even louder to "Jingle Bell Rock". SisQo's eyebrow shot up as he realized just how much stronger her voice had gotten since she was two! She had the talent, that was for sure.

"Where am I?" Elizabeth said, groggily as she came to.

She could feel that she was moving now and the air... it smelled funny.... like Christmas morning. When she opened her eyes, everything was blurry for a half second before everything came into focus. When it did, she felt nauseous again. She looked over the side of the sleigh and saw that they were now hundreds of thousands of feet in the air... nothing but clouds beneath them and at their sides.

"What... is... going... on?" Elizabeth asked, panic rising in her voice.

"She did it," SisQo told her, holding her close to him so that she wouldn't pass out again. "She really did it! We're on our way to the show!"

Elizabeth looked over the side again and then over to her daughter, who was sitting in the very front of the sleigh, leading the way. Seeing her daughter's face light up gave her the warmest feeling inside, and she couldn't help but smile in spite of her fear. Dream or not, yes, her QoQo had done it. She'd done the impossible. She really was a star. She'd made her dreams happen, and Elizabeth couldn't have felt more proud at that moment.

"Put on your seatbelt, Mom!" QoQo shouted over the wind.

Elizabeth looked down and found the cotton-covered belt. When she held it up, she realized that this was what she'd been smelling. It was the sleigh that smelled like Christmas morning. It was just like the smell of pancakes and pine cones from her childhood Christmases. It made her heart swell to double its original size in one single moment. And for the first time since this night has begun, she sat back and relaxed because she has to admit... this was turning out to be the best night of her life.

"So why couldn't we travel to wherever we're going by radio like we did the first time?" SisQo asked over the stereo and QoQo's singing, which he was starting to notice had a good tone.

"Dad! Do you know how many mooncakes *this* wish cost me? Sorry, but I only had enough left over for a sleigh ride!"

SisQo and Elizabeth chuckled. Out of all the cool stuff they'd gotten to do as a couple in the spotlight, they had to admit that riding through the air in an open sleigh was a first. Elizabeth hugged QoQo tight and kissed her hair.

"My special baby," she whispered.

But the moment was cut short when all of a sudden, they heard a pitter, then a patter... then a lonnnnngggg SPUTTER and GROAN of the engine.

"What was *that*?!!" Danni cried out.

"Ummm, it sounded like the engine!" screamed Ryu, a horrified look on his face. "I saw this happen in GTO once!"

And he was right. One quick jerk of the sleigh was all they felt before the entire vehicle tipped forward and started to fall straight from the sky.

"Aaaahhhh!" They all yelled out in unison.

They all piled on top of SisQo, holding on for dear life, as they tumbled through clouds and ozone layers. They even had to break through an entire flock of storks on their way to the ground. A light bulb went off in QoQo's head at that precise moment and she reached for the tiny bottle of stardust that she'd had just a few moments before. But when she pulled the bottle out of her pocket, her heart felt like it was ripping out of her chest. Every last grain of the powder had spilled out of the bottle and out of the sleigh. The sight made her entire world collapse.

"I can't see anything... guys, move... over!" SisQo yelled, "I have to get control of the sleigh!"

But it was no use. He didn't know what to do. His family was in grave danger and he didn't know how to fix it while dropping thousands of feet from the air. All of a sudden, he was helpless and he hated that feeling. He was the head of the household... he was supposed to always keep them safe.

But down, down, down they went, screaming all the way.

QoQo panicked, her heart pumping fast and her eyes bulging out to the size of golf balls. She had no idea what to do next. She couldn't believe it was going to end like this. The last thing that flashed through her mind was that if she was going to die now, she was going to scream so loud at Genie Moon once she got up to heaven because... couldn't she tell the future?!

Why hadn't she predicted that this was going to happen?

And quite coincidentally, that's precisely what Genie Moon was thinking to herself at that exact same moment. How had she not seen this tragic end coming up sooner?! She'd gotten so caught up in the millions of wishes she was getting for Christmas Eve, that she forgot to make sure QoQo and her family landed safely at their destination. And now, they were plummeting toward the ground at rapid speed.

Her heart seemed to plunge right along with them. It had been years since she made a mistake... at least one this big. Now an entire family was going to end up seriously hurt or worse if she didn't figure out something fast.

She watched, with her hands full of soon to be falling stars, as the Andrews' sleigh tumbled down through the sky. It was headed straight for the ground, and by her estimates, it only had about ten minutes before it hit. And that would be the end.

Contrary to popular belief, wishing on a falling star really got you nowhere. The way it worked was that those stars you always saw cascading from the heavens were filled with wishes that had already been granted. Once they hit their target, the wishes manifested on earth. Wishing on one of those was like wishing on a gift that had been wrapped and addressed to someone else long before you ever laid eyes on it. No matter how hard you wished, it would never be yours.

And tonight, there were thousands of falling stars. Over the last month, Genie had granted so many wishes and wrapped them all inside magic stardust to send back down to earth. And she'd thought she had all night to carefully send them to the nice little boys and girls that had wished throughout the year. But she'd have to do a rush job if she wanted to save the Andrews. And of course, she had no choice. It was her fault that they were in trouble in the first place, so she had to get it done before it was too late.

So, knowing that she only had a few minutes left, she gathered all of the wishing stars one by one and started to aim them in the direction that they were meant to go. Stars, of course, were made for this and quite naturally, this was their very favorite time of the year because they got to live out their purpose. They were anxious to get out of Genie's hands and into the hearts of the many children waiting below. And on this night, the stars could feel Genie's nerves bubbling up inside her. They knew that it was very important for them to do their parts in helping to find their targets. And so they helped her by jumping out of her arms before she could even throw them.

First, there were dozens of stars jumping head-first into the night air— then, there were hundreds. Suddenly, thousands could be seen lighting up the night sky like a fountain of dreams. It only took about 30 seconds for them all to get on their way, and it warmed Genie's heart like never before to know that they would band together to help her this way. All she could do was smile at the beautiful sight of wishes literally coming true all around her.

And when it was done, she turned back toward the falling sleigh, where the Andrews family was coming to terms with the fact that they would not make it to see another Christmas.

Everyone was thinking something different. They all knew that the ground was getting closer and closer. They all knew that the end seemed to be near. But none of them thought that there was anything they could do about it. Their stomachs seemed like they were up to their eyeballs and tears filled each of their eyes. But SisQo and Elizabeth were thinking how, if this was their last night on Earth, at least they were together. They hugged their kids tighter inside the sleigh and really tried to stay calm in spite of their fear. Ryu thought that this was how most superheroes went out and he was OK with that. Danni and Juice were thinking that they'd both seen the world and done exactly what they were put on this earth to do and so they could accept their fates.

But QoQo was thinking something very, very different.

She was the only one that knew Genie Moon— you know, really, REALLY knew her. And at that moment, she was thinking that there was no way in the entire world that this was over. Her eyes were glued to the firework show that was going on above their heads. She'd studied the sky enough in the last few weeks to know when there was magic underway. And those lights, she knew, meant that something was happening.

"Everybody, hold on!" she screamed above the rushing wind that was surrounding them.

She saw tears in everyone's eyes and she wanted to tell them not to worry, but she knew there was no use. They didn't believe in magic the way she did. And so she decided that she would have to have enough faith for all of them.

She fixed her eyes on the light above, the stars and the glowing light coming from Genie herself. They were much too far away from her now to see her face, but she knew that Genie could still hear her. So, slowly and carefully, QoQo unbuckled herself from the sleigh's seat and turned around so that she had a full view of the night sky behind them.

"Kimiqo!" her mother was yelling, "Sit down! Please!"

But for the first time in her entire life, she simply ignored her mother. This was too important. So when she was perfectly positioned, she closed her eyes and whispered one last wish for the night. And this time, she didn't have to wait to find out if Genie had heard her or not. Instantly, as if on cue, three stars appeared out of nowhere and surrounded the sleigh, forming a triangle around them.

In one split second, they created a huge bubble between them. It looked like some kind of translucent airbag, and about 30 seconds later, the stars' magic encased them and set them afloat. Looking up at that very moment, QoQo could swear that she caught a wink from above. But just as quickly as she saw it, the sleigh was floating rather quickly off in the direction of about a hundred blinding lights. They were safe inside of the bubble, but they heard shouts and jeers coming from the very direction that they were floating in.

No matter how scary it was to be floating through the pitch black sky toward a landing spot that could be dangerous, they had no choice but to sit tight and wait for whatever Genie had in store for them next.

But Genie was having a bit of trouble of her own. The magic in her fingers was starting to clog up like an old bathroom sink. Where it usually flowed easily out of her, it was stopping short every time she tried to use it. She'd fully intended to send the Andrews another Ooober Sleigh, but she just couldn't conjure up enough magic. The emergency airbag was all she'd been able to manage. And so all she could do was watch from above as they floated lower and lower into what she knew would be a sticky situation.

But the Andrews had no idea just how sticky things were about to get.

Almost like the helium inside a balloon, the air inside the bubble was making them all feel as light as air as the sleigh started to slowly make its ways toward earth. The cheers they'd heard moments before were getting louder, and they could hear that some of the voices weren't cheers at all. About half of the voices were angry and words like "...crush you!" and "...eat you alive!" were starting to float into their bubble.

QoQo, who had been so excited that Genie had stepped in, now started to shrink down into her seat in fright. This wasn't part of the plan. They were supposed to land safely and wait for another sleigh to pick them up. Then, it was off to Hollywood. There weren't supposed to be any monsters between here and her stage.

But then again, there weren't supposed to be any issues with the sleigh in the first place. And it was never supposed to take this long to get there. They were facing the possibility of being late for the show, AND now, they were running into more problems. But QoQo decided that monsters were where she drew the line. There was no way she could fight anything big and scary. This was a job for her father, she thought to herself. And she grabbed his arm, pulled it up, and stuffed her face into his side.

She felt the warmth of his jacket on her face and the comforting rise and fall of his breaths. And even as the grunts and mean words kept coming from down below, her daddy was making her feel safe... for now.

At the same time, SisQo was squinting to see what lay ahead. He could hear all of the yelling and crazy remarks, but of course, he knew there were no monsters. No, whatever it was that was making those sounds was human. In fact, it sounded like a whole lot of humans. And in his mind, it was a good thing. At this point, after hours of only talking to a moon that came alive in the nighttime… and his family who seemed to be hallucinating with him… he needed contact with other people. He needed to know what was going on outside of the bubble they were currently in… literally.

Maybe this was all a dream, he thought.

He thought about all of the dreams he'd had before where a sudden noise or change of scenery meant that he was about to wake up. *How amazing would it be*, he kept thinking, *to wake up on Christmas morning, eat breakfast, and open gifts.* Then, they would laugh and laugh about the crazy dream he'd had where there were talking moons and magic stardust.

But as they got closer and closer, SisQo realized that he was no closer to waking up from this dream than he was when they left the house.

In fact, it was just about to get a lot more interesting.

As they got closer to earth, they all started to realize that the cheers they'd heard were coming from what looked like a huge bowl-like building. The bright lights, the cheers… it was all coming from this huge… open stadium. If the sign that read "Levi's Stadium" was any indication, they were in San Francisco where the Minnesota Vikings were playing the 49ers at that very second. And though they tried to deny it, it looked like they were flying straight toward the middle of it. Down, down, down, the sleigh drifted until it reached the hot spotlights surrounding the plush, green football field.

"Oh, my God… we're going to land right in the middle of the game!" Elizabeth screamed, "SisQo, DO SOMETHING!"

TILESHA BROWN & SISQO

But SisQo didn't see what he *could* do. No one had any
control over where they landed. If that had been the case, they
could have corrected course a long time ago. But SisQo dared
not say that to his wife who was now clinging to him just like
QoQo. He could barely move with them holding tightly to both
of his arms, but he managed to nestle both their heads in the
cradle of his arms while he reached for the reins in front of him.
There was no horse or reindeer to guide, but just holding them
made him a little less anxious.

Down below, little specks of people were scurrying to
and fro like little ants as the sleigh got closer and closer. He
could just make out the colors on each team's uniforms and at
least two black and white striped figures on the field. He thought
to himself that they looked like zebras from way up high, but he
knew they were referees. And seeing them gave him an idea.

"You're making a *phone call*??" Elizabeth screeched as
they continued to drift toward the football field. It was now only
about 15,000 feet away.

SisQo didn't answer. Instead, he simply finished dialing
the number and pressed the phone up to his ear.

The phone rang. And rang. And rang.

SisQo's heart sank. He'd never needed someone to
answer the phone so badly in his entire life. They were getting
closer and closer to the stadium and any minute, they were
going to barrel right through the game and the players on the
field.

He needed to warn someone. Anyone.

"Hello? SisQo?" the animated voice boomed through the
phone seconds later. "Hey!!! How's it going?"

"Very fast! It's going very fast!" SisQo was yelling into

* 60 *

the phone.

He couldn't believe his friend had answered on the very *last* ring.

"Whoa, whoa! What's wrong, man?"

"Coming straight... for... Levi's... Stadium!" SisQo's voice shot into the mouthpiece.

Several feet away, sitting as close as you could possibly get to the field was a group of five guys, munching on popcorn and watching the field eagerly.

"Levi's! Yeah, how'd you know we were here?"

The men were sitting with a tub of freshly buttered popcorn, a tray of hot dogs, and cold cans of soda surrounding them like a ballgame buffet. The man on the phone sat with his face scrunched and his phone jammed to his ear trying to hear over the roaring fans all around him.

"Listen to me," SisQo's voice came through the phone, "I'm here…but I'm in trouble. I need you to get the referees to stop the game. Get all the players off the field! Then, we need something to land on!"

"SisQo, I can barely hear you, man…," the man was screaming into the receiver. "It sounds like you said you want me to stop the game? I'm not gamin' right now, man… I'm at a real live *FOOTBALL* game."

He gave a little snort of laughter as he said the words, confusion and amusement dancing on his face at the same time. He and SisQo had become friends because of their love of video games, but he'd have to play with him later. The fans were shouting way too loudly and he could hardly even hear him.

"You *have* to listen to me! I'm at the game too! And we need some place to land!"

SisQo's voice was frantic now. They were feet away from the ground and the wind was carrying them right into center field. The lower they floated to earth, the more directly they drifted toward the center of the game's action. They only had about 1,000 more feet to drop before they were officially inside the stadium's dome.

It only took seconds for people to notice them and start to stare... then point... and all of a sudden, the chants began to sound different. The screams died down to a buzz of murmurs as they tried to figure out if what they were seeing was actually real.

Could it be? A floating bubble with a... sleigh inside?

And who was in there? It looked like an entire group of people.

You could almost feel the fear rolling like a wave through the thousands of people standing up in the stands, watching. But it didn't compare to the fear that SisQo and his family were feeling inside. Everyone was looking at them. It felt like a dream... like the ones where you're standing in front of your classroom without clothes or where you're flying through the sky and then start to fall.

Again, SisQo wished this was a dream. Then, all he'd have to do was wake up. His mind drifted back to the smell of breakfast cooking and his kids screaming for joy as they started to open their presents. For just an instant, he heard a tiny voice in the back of his mind telling him that he wasn't being real with himself, though. If he were honest, if QoQo hadn't brought him through that radio, he would've woken up tomorrow morning in a hotel room... alone... with nothing to comfort him but room service. And his kids... he looked at each one of them and then his wife.... they would've been alone too.

The realization of what this night meant to all of them hit him all in a flash. This is why this had had to happen. He needed to learn exactly what was at stake every minute he wasn't with his family. He hadn't ever thought about it that way before, so now he was about to learn the hard way. With that thought in his mind, he took on a new strength and new confidence. He would not let this crazy moment get the better of him. No matter what he had to do, he had to get QoQo to that show… and not just so that he could get his talent back… but to show her that he would always be willing to go to the moon and back to show her how much he loved them all.

That meant that even if he had to jump out of a sleigh mid-air to save them from crashing onto a football field— as bizarre as that sounded— that was what he would do. So, he started to unbuckle his seatbelt and unbutton his coat.

"What are you doing?!" Elizabeth screamed.

And QoQo clung to her father like she never had before.

"I have to jump!" SisQo said over the rushing wind.

"What??!!" Elizabeth's face was twisted in confusion and shock that he would even think about leaving them to do something so crazy.

"Trust me… I got this," SisQo said, grabbing both sides of her face.

They only had about three minutes before the sleigh reached the ground, but he knew he had to use some of it to tell his family how much he loved them. He didn't know what would happen to either of them, and he needed them to know. He needed to say the words.

"I love you all," he said, kissing Elizabeth and then each one of the kids, "You're the best thing that has ever happened to me."

"But"— Elizabeth sputtered through falling tears.

"You'll tell Shai, right?" he asked Elizabeth about his oldest daughter, "that I love her so much?"

All Elizabeth could do was nod as tears rolled down her cheeks.

She tried to reach out her hand to stop him, but before she could grab hold of him, SisQo had jumped out of the sleigh, tucked his body in and was tumbling through the air toward the ground. Elizabeth and both kids covered their eyes until they heard the crowd take in a collective gasp all at once. And even then, all Elizabeth could do was move one finger from her eye so that she could peer out onto the field.

And when she did, there she saw her husband, now a crumpled up body lying right at the 50-yard mark.

And he wasn't moving.

What Elizabeth couldn't see was that SisQo was, in fact, breathing. Shallow and ragged, his breaths were coming out in short bursts of air, but he was alive. And a few moments later, he just managed to lift his head up to try to figure out how badly he was hurt. Imaginary stars started to spin around his head and the earth seemed to shake a little beneath him. But all he could think was to shout to the referee.

The next thing he knew, he heard about a dozen

footsteps galloping in his direction, and he started to mumble something under his breath. His voice was barely above a whisper at first, but as they got closer, a supernatural strength filled his lungs, and he managed to push out exactly two strong syllables just as a pair of black shoes came into view.

"SAVE THEM!"

And when the man standing in front of him heard the words, he paused only for a second before looking up, understanding creeping up into his face. And then, he jumped into action. Before SisQo could even blink twice, there was a blowing of a whistle, several feet clamoring away, and about a dozen voices yelling one word: FOAM!

Up above, the sleigh was coming down steadily with no sign of stopping or slowing down. Everyone in the crowd had their eyes glued on the sinking bubble. You could almost feel the anticipation in the air. Everyone wanted to know what it was and what would happen once it reached the ground.

SisQo closed his eyes for precisely 10 seconds before he decided that he simply had to get up. No matter how much pain he was in, no matter how much he couldn't even believe that all of this was happening— he had to get up and help make sure the sleigh had somewhere to land. His whole entire life…. his very heart… was in that bubble and he needed to make sure that they weren't hurt.

Slowly, slowly, he got to his feet just in time to see the entire Minnesota Vikings football team scrambling to pull a foam landing pad from the tunnel across the field. The announcer was shouting into the speaker system overhead trying to tell fans to keep calm all over the stadium. But no one was listening. This was literally a once-in-a-lifetime event— far more interesting than a football game. And now they were excited.

Flashes went off as everyone pointed their phones to the sky, taking pictures and posting to their social media pages. Even the stadium workers started to take advantage of their cameras, using the jumbotron to zoom in on the man that had fallen from the sky... AKA SisQo, who was now on his feet and staring around the stadium. He met the eyes of thousands of fans pointing at him and all of a sudden, he felt the energy shift.

They recognized him.

He heard the hushed whispers of people saying his name with increasing excitement. They were pointing with a purpose now and he could almost feel the hashtags starting to go viral. But even with all of the attention focused on him, he turned toward the sleigh that was now making its way straight for the foam bed that the players had placed on the field to catch it. It was like a huge mattress that pole vaulters use to land after they jump. It was genius, really... the way they'd jumped into action and knew exactly what he'd needed them to do.

The entire Vikings team had rallied together to save his family and he couldn't think of any moment in his life that he'd felt more grateful.

"Thank God," SisQo whispered.

And tears formed in his eyes as the sleigh fell down, down, down, and landed with a soft but forceful thud onto the soft foam. And when it did, a silence fell over the entire stadium. SisQo looked around, not knowing what to do. But within moments, he was gathering all of the strength that he still had left in his body and using it to push himself toward the sleigh.

It took everything within him to get to them and leap onto the super-sized mattress where his family was. Usually, people needed a 15-foot pole to get to the top of one of these, but he felt like Superman tonight. He could and would do anything for his family. It seemed like he'd only blinked but suddenly, he was at the sleigh, holding his entire family within his arms.

"Don't you ever do anything like that again!" Elizabeth was screaming at him through heavy drops of tears, "We thought— we thought"—

"Shhh… it's ok," SisQo said pulling her head to his chest, "It's OK. I'm OK."

And they all held him a little tighter for the next several seconds. But it didn't last longer than that because a strange noise was starting to rise up from the crowd just then. They didn't know exactly what it was at first, but when they popped their heads up and really started to listen… their hearts froze. It wasn't really a noise. They were… voices. An entire sea of people was now chanting in a very low tone.

"SisQo! SisQo!"

And then the sound of a foghorn and the voice of an announcer was blaring over the loudspeaker.

"SisQo… is that *really* you?"

The voice came out loud and its echo bounced around the stadium. SisQo let out a huge sigh, then slowly got up from the place he'd been kneeling. And when he turned around to face the crowd, he forced a little smile before nodding very slowly. He hoped that they just wanted to acknowledge him or—

But he didn't have a chance to finish that thought because thunderous applause spread throughout the stadium at that very second. When he looked up, he saw kids and moms and dads all over the stadium on their feet, clapping like he'd just scored a touchdown. It didn't all click at once, but the longer he stood there taking it all in, the more he started to understand. The world had never seen him like this. They knew him as a singer— even an actor. But he'd never been seen as a true family man… or… could it be even more than that? Could they be seeing him as a…

"You're a hero," he heard Elizabeth whisper into his ear from behind him.

And another look around at the faces staring back at him confirmed it. He hadn't really thought about what he was doing at the moment. He'd just jumped into action. And now he didn't know how to feel. Proud? Invincible?

No.

He just felt… appreciative.

One by one, he turned and brought each of his kids and his wife to stand beside him as the crowd continued to clap. It felt like it was never going to end. People everywhere were beaming and hugging their own families. It was literally the most beautiful moment they'd ever experienced.

But suddenly, they could all feel it coming to an end when they felt the foam shake beneath their feet. And when SisQo turned around, there was a tall man with greedy eyes and short brown hair that framed his face, which at the moment had a broad smile and a suspicious expression plastered on it. He wore a crisp suit and he stood stiffly, just staring at him before he shouted into the microphone that he was holding in his hand.

"SisQo!" he bellowed as he moved closer to the entire Andrews family. "Nice of you to… drop in!"

He was smiling and kind of singing his words, but there was something else going on behind his eyes. SisQo didn't say anything for a long while because he was trying to figure out exactly why the man was looking at him the way he was. And why was he talking to him with a microphone? Did he want an interview?

SisQo could hardly think with the pain from the fall setting in and sending lightning-like sensations through his entire body with every breath. So instead of trying to figure out anything else, he turned to try to get down from the foam mountain. It would be much more difficult to get down now that he was coming down from superhero mode. But all he could think about was getting out of there.

"I was just leaving," he said to the man as he turned around to gain his balance and help his family off the landing pad after him.

"No! No, no, no, no!" the man said, making SisQo stop dead in his tracks. "You can't *leave!*"

"Come again?" SisQo whispered.

And again, the man shouted into the microphone in a booming radio voice for the entire stadium to hear.

"I think the people would love to hear a few words... or maybe even a song..." the man sang the words, grinning at the crowd now., "Isn't that right?"

The words seemed to drip out of his mouth like dirty grease, and there was just something about him that couldn't be trusted. SisQo stared at him, literally not blinking, for several seconds. And suddenly, he knew what this was about. All of these people... the drama with the sleigh... the suspense... the victory. And now him being a celebrity just put the icing on the cake. All of it equaled money... for this guy in a suit. Millions of people were tuning in right now. Millions of families in their homes were seeing this all happen on their television screens. It all spelled out hard, cold cash for this guy. Advertisers were going to be blowing up his phone and this team would be worth more money than he could ever even imagine by tomorrow morning.

"Let me guess... you're the owner of the team?" SisQo shot back in a cold tone.

"Close," the man said, not speaking into the microphone for the first time. "It's just a simple favor. I'm guessing you still need to get home. And I doubt you have what you need... in *there*."

The man shot a glance over at the sleigh, now broken down and torn apart. Out of the corner of his eye, SisQo saw his cell phone still laying on the field, smashed and broken.

"Oh, we can get back home," SisQo said, anger starting to rise in his voice. "I don't need you or anybody else— "

But just as he was about to finish, he felt Elizabeth touch his side like she always did when he was about to go too far.

"We have nothing," she whispered to him. "No cell phones, no money, no nothing. We're in our pajamas, for Christ's sake!"

And it was true. All except for SisQo and his dancers, they'd all been awakened out of their sleep and tossed into a magical sleigh. There was no way to get home... except through this throng of people, who SisQo was just now starting to realize were chanting again. Now that this man had mentioned it... these people were expecting a show, and they didn't look like they'd take no for an answer.

"We want SisQo! We want SisQo!"

All over the stadium, the chant was getting louder and louder as more and more people chimed in. There was no way out of this. If he left now, he'd lose his status as a hero quicker than you could say "Unleash the Dragon." But what could he do? There was still the issue of him not having his talent anymore. He literally didn't have it in him to perform even if he wanted to. He'd never been in this position before. He'd been singing since he was two years old…. ever since he could hold a microphone.

This was painful. His heart actually hurt at the thought of not being able to do the thing he felt like he was on this very earth to do. But then, it occurred to him. He *had* traded that talent for something else. And as if he and Elizabeth had been thinking the exact same thing at the exact same moment, they both shot a sidelong glance over at their baby girl, sitting impatiently on the edge of the mess that used to be a sleigh.

Small butterflies were growing bigger and bigger inside QoQo's stomach. She knew this was coming. She'd been watching this whole scene unfold in sheer horror. They wanted her father to sing and it was her fault that he couldn't. And she didn't trust the look in that man's eyes. She couldn't quite put her finger on it, but she had the sense that this could all go very wrong, very fast. And now her parents were looking at her with such fear on their faces.

So instead of letting them be the ones to ask, she stood up and blurted out two words before they could even open their mouths.

"I'm ready," QoQo said.

And her face told them that she meant it. Her tone told them that she meant it. Even her eyes said she was ready.

But after it was all worked out, it was agreed that she would be the one making her debut. SisQo and the guys would be her backup dancers, and according to everyone there, this was going to be the cutest thing to ever grace the stadium's stage. But at the end of the day, QoQo worried that she was not, in fact, ready for this.

Her stomach was doing flips and those small butterflies that had been flapping inside of her just a few minutes before were now full-grown and were making her feel nauseous. She shouldn't have eaten all of those mooncakes, she thought to herself. But still, she refused to let fear show up on her face. She never said a word as the owner called an early emergency halftime or as the stadium workers set up a stage the size of the entire field for the entire crowd to see. She didn't even say anything when they dressed her in one of the tutus that had been meant for the show originally scheduled for the Christmas parade the next day.

She… never… said…a… word.

A young woman came to get QoQo to take her onto the big stage after about half an hour. She seemed nice enough. Her blonde hair was wrapped into a neat bun and she wore glasses that sat on the edge of her nose. She was dressed in simple black pants, a white shirt, and black high-heeled shoes. And there was a black headset attached to her ear that she kept getting instructions from.

While she waited for QoQo to get last minute touches, she kept talking into the headset to someone no one could hear, but she stopped every so often to smile at Elizabeth and SisQo. They guessed it was to set their minds at ease, but it wasn't working. The longer they looked at QoQo's long face, the more nervous they became.

"She doesn't look so good," Elizabeth whispered to SisQo.

And she was right. QoQo's face was turning an odd shade of green and she still wasn't saying anything to anyone as the woman took her by the hand and led her out onto the field. SisQo and Elizabeth watched as they went.

"What do we do?" SisQo asked, worry creeping up into his eyes, "I'm gonna just call the whole thing off."

He said it so abruptly that Elizabeth barely had time to react. Before she knew it, he was running after QoQo as they climbed the iron stairs to the top of the stage. Before he could reach her, though, what looked like a dozen hands swooped her up off the top iron landing and placed her on the mega stage. And everything went way too quickly from there.

The lights clicked on overhead, flooding the stage and there QoQo stood... looking out into the sea of faces staring back at her. Her eyes blinked wildly until she got used to the brightness of the field lights and then she nearly jumped out of her skin when a piano began to play behind her.

SisQo could see the utter shock and fear on his daughter's face, and he couldn't help himself. He flew up onto the stage to stand beside her. A flood of applause erupted from the crowd as soon as he did and at that moment, he realized that he didn't have a plan. He couldn't help her sing. He didn't know if he could dance or not. Had Genie taken his dance moves too? He didn't know what to do at all, so he just stood there like a reindeer in headlights. Everyone was staring, and neither he nor QoQo could manage to move a muscle.

That is until they heard the light tap of footsteps on the stage just behind them. They couldn't look. They couldn't move, but only five seconds later, they saw a shadow come to stand beside QoQo, and a familiar voice floated over their frozen bodies.

"I got this," it was Ryu talking, "Don't worry, sis."

They saw him point toward the back of the stage at someone, and all of a sudden, a fast-paced song was blaring over the speakers. The lights went out dramatically, then came back up!

What was Ryu doing? SisQo wondered.

But then, he saw for himself when one single spotlight came up seconds later, and Ryu was glowing right in the center of it. With the attention off of them, QoQo and SisQo began to relax and back into the shadows where they could really see Ryu move.

They glanced at the crowd to see if they noticed them moving off the stage, but every eye was glued to Ryu. SisQo's jaw dropped as his son started pop-locking for several minutes, then began gliding from one end of the stage to the other in a flawless moonwalk. Then, as the beat dropped hard and started to come to an end, he finished the crowd off with the infamous flash spin that his dad had taught him. At the end of the spin, he landed in a perfect split.

Offstage, SisQo couldn't blink. He simply could not believe what he was seeing. He had seen Ryu dance around the house and even at the occasional show when he let him come up on stage with him, but this was a perfectly choreographed routine that he had to have practiced in his room about a million times before tonight. It was *that* good!

But he wasn't about to get the chance to tell Ryu how great he'd done just yet, because right at that moment, Ryu was holding out his hand to his sister. He was telling her to come out on stage with him with his hands, and his eyes were saying that he would make everything ok.

A warmth filled SisQo's heart right then. It was the same

thing he'd felt earlier. He knew that something was happening to his family on this night. And it felt amazing.

QoQo must have agreed because she took one step and then another. The crowd roared again when they saw her stepping into the spotlight next to her brother. And in just an instant, Ryu had QoQo by the band, spinning her in a circle all around him. At first, it took her by surprise but being there, dancing with her brother helped her feel as light as air. She dared not open her mouth to sing, but she could move like this forever. Her tiny body was twirling just like a ballerina across the stage.

She never let go of Ryu's hand, but she found the rhythm with him. And she felt a big wave of magic rise up inside of her as they took over the stage. Little did they both know, SisQo was feeling it too. He motioned for Juice and Danni to come up to the stage, and when they were beside him, he whispered for them to take their places behind the two kids who were magically mixing hip-hop dance with classical ballet in a way that he'd never seen before.

And that reminded him of something.

Some of his favorite songs that he'd written had the same balance. So as Juice and Danni fell in line, playing off the kids, SisQo made his way to the band and had them start to add strings to the song that was already playing. At first, they frowned up at the thought, but once the guitar was added, they started to understand. And when they'd caught on to the idea that SisQó had, the piano player jumped in to add a light melody. And then the trumpeter followed. Before they knew it, they had a big band, hip-hop ensemble and the entire crowd was rocking out to a brand new song that they'd just made up on the spot.

Off to the side, the woman with the blonde hair was sitting, staring at the whole ordeal. And it looked like she didn't know whether to smile or cry. SisQo motioned to her, making his hands look like an explosion. Then, he mouthed one word to her: *fireworks*.

At first, she looked like she wanted to refuse, but one look at her boss, the man with the dark hair and hungry eyes, made her jump into action. This was his show, and he would not have any stone unturned. His face said the more fireworks, the merrier.

And from the first burst moments later, everyone all over the entire stadium could feel it... this indescribable feeling that something truly magical was in the air. Before SisQo knew it, QoQo was at his feet, beaming like she'd just won the four-year-old lottery. She was tugging at his pants. And when he looked down from the lights in the sky at his daughter, he saw her motioning for him to stoop down so that she could whisper something to him. His heart wouldn't let him refuse.

He dropped to his knee and leaned in real close so that her tiny hands were cupping his ear.

"This wasn't Genie," her whispers tickled in his ear, "This was *your* magic... the magic *inside* of you!"

And she was right. One look around, SisQo had to admit that even without the talents that Genie had taken from him, there was still something in him. Leave it to QoQo to notice. He was now looking at her in a whole new way. She wasn't the QoQo he thought he knew. She wasn't *just* a little girl, he thought. And he wasn't the only one who was taking notice.

Elizabeth stood back in the crowd, watching proudly. A smile was sneaking up the corners of her mouth as she took in the moment. These were her babies, but they had so much more in them than she'd known. How could she have missed this? And why had she been worried that tonight wouldn't work? Even despite QoQo clamming up, her brother was right there to

SISQO'S PERFECT CHRISTMAS

back her up, and they were just fine up there performing and bringing joy to this entire place. She glanced around and really took in how many people were on their feet, rocking out with her family.

She was lost deep in thought when a tap came at her shoulder. She jumped at the surprise, but when she turned around, she couldn't believe her eyes.

"Oh my— Oh my God... it's"—

She was stuttering and stammering so much that she could hardly catch her breath. But it was like he didn't even notice. He merely smiled and held out his hand.

"Eric— Eric Kendricks. I play for the Vikings."

Elizabeth looked him up and down and then nodded. Of course, he played for the Vikings. He was covered from head to toe in purple and gold. And of course, she knew who he was. Everyone living in Minnesota knew who Eric Kendricks was.

"Ummm," Elizabeth tried to make words come out.

She'd never really been star struck, but Eric Kendricks was such a gem of a person. He was always in the news for doing something charitable, and he was a fantastic role model for her son. And more importantly, she hadn't been expecting to meet him... tonight... like this. This was insane.

"I'm sorry to bother you, but do you think I could get an autograph?"

"Oh! You're a fan of SisQo's?! Yes, I'm sure he'd love to"—

She turned from Eric for just a second to see if she could spot her husband, but he'd already begun to come down off of the stage. Eric's voice stopped her cold.

"No, no— SisQo's great and all," he said, "but those kids of yours… they're stars!"

Shock spread over Elizabeth's face. Her kids were celebrities now? She had to take a minute for that to really sink in. But everything sort of went blank when she caught sight of something in the corner of her eye. There SisQo was, off to the side of the stage arguing with the man with the dark eyes.

SisQo was inches away from his face, and he looked like he might pounce at any minute.

"Hold that thought for just a second," she told Eric.

And then she ran like there was no tomorrow toward the two men. Ryu and QoQo were off to the side screaming for SisQo to stop yelling at the man, but Elizabeth still couldn't figure out what the two men were arguing about. The only thing that reached her ears was the sound of the dark man's command once he'd turned away from SisQo.

"Let them come for him," he said coolly and then walked away.

He'd given this order to the woman with the blonde hair, whose face turned grave once his back was to her. Elizabeth noticed that she seemed to be shaking as she moved toward a man standing guard at the foot of the stage. When she reached him, she whispered one sentence into the man's ear and walked away very nervously.

"What's going on?" Elizabeth whispered to herself.

She'd been frozen in place watching these bizarre people move around. Even the way they walked seemed off somehow. But Elizabeth shook herself back to reality. She needed to get to

SisQo to find out how they were going to get out of there. They'd done their performance, and now she assumed that everyone was getting things planned for them to get to Hollywood and then back home in time for Christmas. And she hoped that the return flight would be in someone's private jet! She didn't think she could take any more sleigh rides.

But that thought vanished from her mind once she actually reached SisQo and looked him in the eye. That strange feeling was back. Something *was* wrong. Her heart sank.

"What is it?" She asked grabbing his hand, "What's wrong?"

"He's got the place blocked off... says we need to do press," SisQo said through clenched teeth. "He said that's the least we can do if we need six plane tickets. I can't believe this! Where's Genie now?!"

The last question hit QoQo like a ton of bricks. She didn't know where Genie was, and she wished more than anything that she would show up right then and there. The magic that had been in the stadium was dwindling by the second. There was something else settling into its place... and it didn't feel good either.

And then she saw it.

"Umm, Daddy," QoQo spun around and pulled on SisQo's coat. "Look!"

They all turned toward the stands closest to them and gasped all at the same time. At that very moment, thousands of people were now coming onto the field in a crazy stampede. And they were headed straight for them!

"Aaahhh!" Elizabeth screamed.

The crowd was yelling about autographs and pictures, but it was pure chaos. When they looked over the tops of their heads, they could see security guards actually ushering the mob of people out of the stands and onto the field.

"It's a setup!" SisQo screamed.

But it was too late. The fans were on their heels and there seemed to be no way to get out of there. They were coming at them from all sides. All of the barricades had been lifted. And they knew that all of the staff had been ordered not to help them.

And just then, they saw the tall frame of Eric Kendrick appear just in front of them.

"Run!" he was shouting, "This way... into the tunnel!"

And they realized that they had no time to ask any questions. They just took off! Poor QoQo couldn't keep up, so Juice had to scoop her into his arms as they made their way across the field. It felt like it took hours instead of just minutes, but they finally reached the tunnel on the opposite end of the stadium. Some of the crowd had gotten tired of running at the halfway mark, but there was still a fair amount of people coming for them when SisQo reached the large opening and ran inside.

"Thanks, man!" SisQo said, shaking Eric's hand.

"Anytime, man," Eric said, "Be careful."

And with that, he pulled the huge metal doors closed behind him. When he was gone, they all breathed a deep sigh of relief together.

"What do we do now?" Danni asked.

"There's gotta be some door that leads to the outside,"

Juice added.

But it was impossible to tell which pathway led to safety in the darkness of the tunnel. And they didn't have much time. Any minute now, all of those people would be funneling into that tunnel looking for them, so they had to think of something.

"Lord, help us, " SisQo said, and he genuinely looked afraid and exhausted all at the same time.

Through the darkness, QoQo saw her father's face drop like he was defeated. She just couldn't believe that all of this had been for nothing. They'd been through so much in only one night. This was so unfair. Where was Genie? That was the one thing she'd been counting on… the magic. And now, it seemed to be gone forever.

Just as she was thinking of all the things she should've done differently since she'd met Genie, something lit up down the hall to their right, at the very end of the tunnel. No one was sure what they were looking at, but it seemed to be the headlights of a car. That didn't seem right, did it? Could a car drive down here? They all wondered if they were finally just losing it after this long and crazy night.

But no.

There was definitely something there. A car… or something. And it was definitely headed straight for them. Part of SisQo wanted to yell to them all to run in the opposite direction. For all he knew, this could have been more fans coming to mow him down for an autograph or picture. But he was too tired now. All of them were too exhausted to move. They all silently agreed that this was where it ended. They weren't running anymore. This was it.

And as the car-looking thing slowly emerged out of the darkness and moved closer and closer toward them… they realized that it wasn't a car at all. It was a—

"Golf cart?" Ryu asked, breaking the silence.

"Yep!" said a voice from behind the steering wheel. "And we've come to take you home!"

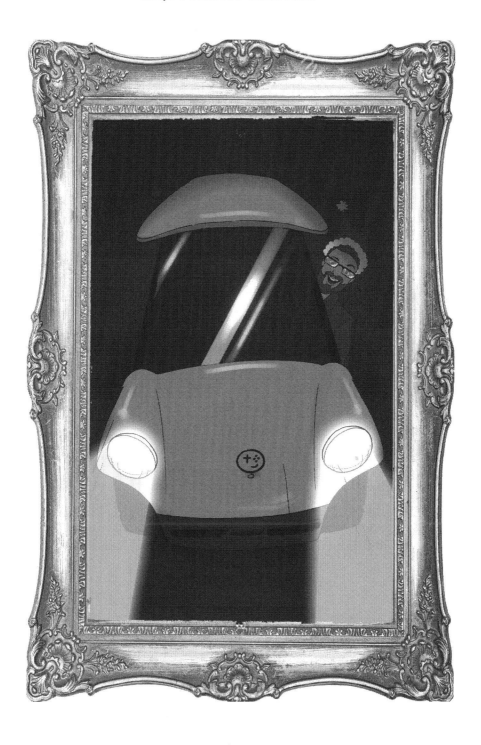

There was a long pause as SisQo tried to put all of these pieces together. The cart, the voice, the face that was slowly coming into view. It was the man that SisQo had called while he was crashing into the football stadium.

"Greg?!" SisQo asked, completely confused.

The cart came to a complete stop at their feet, and they realized that it wasn't just Greg. Nick was there, too... and so were Tim, Kevin, Andy, Joey, and even Cool Greg hanging on to the back. This was the entire Kinda Funny podcast crew— SisQo's favorite podcast! They were there to save them.

"Sorry we didn't understand earlier," Greg said, "It was so *wild* to see you land out there on the field! I mean, man, you were— "

"It's ok, it's ok... listen, we really need to get out of here," SisQo said looking over his shoulder, "Can you give us a ride?"

"Of course! That's what we're here for," Nick yelled, "Get on!"

Before they knew it, they were all packed into this mysteriously stretchy golf cart. From the outside, it didn't look like they should all fit, but they did. And before they could ask any questions, they were rushing off into the blackness of the tunnel ahead of them. Their cheeks were nearly blasted off of their faces they were going so fast, and it seemed like all they did was blink and they were out of the tunnel, burning serious rubber through the streets of San Francisco, with no clue where they were headed next.

4

Crashing Through the Snow?!

"A mega-rider- cross sensational- what???" SisQo asked.

Greg sighed.

"It's a mega-watt, carbon-fiber, snappy flex, twin-directional Aerocart," he said calmly.

They were all back at the Kinda Funny studio looking at either the most fantastic contraption they'd ever seen or the most ridiculous one. Neither SisQo nor Elizabeth could make up their minds which. But despite the looks on their faces, Greg was still trying his best to explain that it was the only way to get QoQo to the performance in Hollywood on time.

"It's a time traveler," Nick chimed in to try to convince SisQo, "Jump in, get a running start, push the button, and arrive at whatever time you want at the destination you choose."

"Sweet!" Ryu exclaimed.

But Elizabeth clinched her hand tighter around QoQo and Ryu.

"Is it... safe?" she asked.

"Of course, it's sa"—

"Well..."

All of a sudden, Nick punched Greg playfully in the ribs and Greg sighed.

"Truthfully... we have no idea," Greg admitted.

Elizabeth suddenly looked like she wanted to make a run for it.

"SisQo, we can't... we shouldn't..."

"But Mom! We'll never make it in time to get Dad's talent back." QoQo piped up, "We gotta go now... we just gotta!"

SisQo and Elizabeth looked at each other and shook their heads in agreement. Silently, they decided that it would be too much of a risk. They'd already been through enough. So Elizabeth turned to QoQo and put her hand on either side of her face.

"It's too dangerous, baby girl" she whispered, tears stinging her eyelids, "We have to go home now. We'll catch the bus or try to get a flight— this is all too much."

"But"— Greg caught himself and seemed to decide not to argue anymore. "Alright, alright. I won't force it."

"It's too late to book a flight," SisQo said, sadness ringing in his voice. "Any bus stations around?"

"Well, I think this is how it works..." QoQo's voice

came slowly from behind them.

And when they turned around, they couldn't believe their eyes. QoQo had been writing on a giant chalkboard for the last several seconds, but no one paid her any attention because they thought she'd just been scribbling. You know, the way kids do. But now, as they looked closer, they saw that these weren't scribbles at all. They were plans. And figures. And drawings... very complicated drawings.

"What are they?" asked Juice.

"This is how it works," QoQo repeated.

And sure enough, as they followed the chart that she'd drawn with their eyes, they slowly figured out that everything on the board came together to explain the engine of the Aerocart perfectly. And it described it in a way that they could understand.

"So, basically... the engine makes it possible for the wind coming in from all sides to lift the cart into the air?" SisQo asked.

QoQo nodded, grinning.

"And because it's using all of the air as a force, it forms a bubble around the cart keeping everyone safe, right?" Juice asked next.

"Mmm-hmm!" QoQo said excitedly.

"And what does that mark mean right there?"

Danni pointed to a star-like symbol just below QoQo's drawing of the Aerocart's tailpipe.

"Oh, that's our manufacturer's logo," Greg said casually, "She's big on symbols."

Greg rolled his eyes as he said this, but Ryu's lit up! He almost fell off the chair that he was sitting on. Recognition was all over his face and he just... stared for more than a couple of seconds without even blinking.

"What is it, Ryu?" Elizabeth asked, panic just on the edge of her tongue.

"*She*...made it," Ryu almost whispered it. He was in such disbelief.

"Who?"

It was like they all asked in unison— all of them on the edges of their seats.

"Genie."

And hearing the name, Cool Greg smacked his lips from the corner of the room.

"Oh yeah, that's her," he said with a shrug. "She assembled it, but *we* were the brains behind the science."

He puffed his chest out proudly. They couldn't help but be proud of themselves. They were so creative. They'd done so much in their careers and this was certainly an invention for the books. But SisQo knew that there could be just a little more to this story and he couldn't help but ask questions.

"And you're absolutely sure it's *all* science and not..." SisQo didn't finish the sentence.

He didn't want to hurt the guys' feelings. It was just that he'd seen so much tonight. He'd learned that there was much more out there than he ever knew existed. And seeing Genie's symbol on the Aerocart kind of made him trust it a bit more. He knew Greg was smart... genius even... but he knew that Genie could *fly*.

He knew that if he put his family in a golf cart that Genie built, they'd get there in one piece. Even the sleigh she'd sent them was covered by a magical airbag. And in the end, it had saved them.

"Not what?" Greg asked, his ears perking up.

SisQo looked down and fiddled with his hands awkwardly.

"Magic?!" Ryu shouted.

Everyone turned to SisQo and he couldn't help himself. A wide grin started to spread across his face. He was feeling much more confident now that he knew that Genie was behind the contraption. He didn't understand why he still trusted her, but he did. He supposed that it had something to do with the fact that he felt like he'd known her his whole life. She'd always been there— the moon— hanging up there watching down over them all. And tonight, she might not have gotten them to Hollywood straight away, but she'd helped them discover the true meaning of family, love, and Christmas, nonetheless.

Now, he was finding out that she'd made this time and distance traveler and for some reason, he knew in his heart that it would work. This was the end of all of their obstacles. With this thing, they could be on their way to Hollywood to get his talents back in no time. Yes, his talents. He had missed them, especially now when this night had been so full of magic. He heard QoQo tell him that he still had magic inside of him back on the field, but it sure didn't feel like it when he was around men with flying time machines and his kids who were now celebrities in their own right.

"Dad, we have to go now," Ryu said, "Let's go or QoQo's gonna be late!"

And looking down at his watch, SisQo saw that he was right. Even though he was very relieved that they hadn't missed the show, he was surprised to see that it was only 10:30. The disaster at the stadium had seemed to go on forever. But even though it wasn't quite midnight yet, they did need to get out of there... so he got his things together.

"Uh, SisQo, can I talk to you for a second," Elizabeth asked in a flat, low tone, "in *private?*"

He knew this wasn't going to go well, but he followed her into the hallway anyway. He knew she had her doubts and he had to hear her out. That was only fair. On the other hand, however, they were in a huge hurry. He hoped he could convince her in record time.

But as soon as they were in the hallway, away from everyone, her face told him that she would *not* be easy to sway.

"SisQo, did you forget that you just had to jump out of a crashing sleigh just a few hours ago? And now you want to put you, me, and your kids into a *flying golf cart?* Have you lost your mind?!"

SisQo just stared at her. She always had a way of spelling things out in a way that he hadn't seen on his own, he thought. And what could he say? It *was* dangerous. It *was* risky. He had gotten really hurt in the sleigh accident. That much, he could admit. But there was still a nagging feeling in the back of his mind that it had happened for a reason. It had brought them all closer and he loved that. And when he really thought about it, Genie had opened all of their eyes to the possibilities of magic touching real life. And he never wanted to go back. In fact, he wanted to keep trying new things. He was ready for adventure.

"It's not practical," Elizabeth said aloud, breaking up SisQo's thoughts, "Let's just go home...the *regular* way!"

Just as she said those words, Kevin and Joey came rushing toward them with worried looks on their faces.

"Yo, what's wrong?" SisQo asked, "What happened?"

But neither one of them answered. Instead, Andy stood in the middle of the room like he'd just seen a ghost.

"It's the kids," Andy said, his chest rising and falling hard beneath his shirt, "They're gone!"

5

I'll Be Toast for Christmas

Exactly one hour before the kids went missing, Genie was planning a disappearance of her own. She had been shaken to her core by what was happening with the Andrews family. Never in the whole history of her career had she failed as miserably as she had on this Christmas Eve. Never in her life had she felt her magic slipping away the way it was this night. So now that they were safe with the Kinda Funny crew, she had to slip away to visit an old friend.

Well, he wasn't exactly a friend, but he was the only one she knew who still possessed what the heavens called a Mooncharge. It was something that she was not allowed to own because no magical being in the universe could possess anything that would make their powers more powerful than anyone else's. It was Lunar Law that all powers be created equal.

And so, Genie prepared to come down from her heavenly perch. Before leaving, she hung a life-size portrait of herself in the sky where the moon should have been. It would serve as her placeholder until she got back. She'd answered every wish for the night, so anyone looking for her could find her when she returned. There was something more urgent that she needed to take care of.

Now, it's important to know that the moon did not leave her home to go to Earth very often, but when she did, she liked to do it in human form. Could you imagine seeing a big ball of angelic light just rolling through towns on earth? She would be all over the six o'clock news before she could even make it to her destination.

No, it was easier to go as a human. And she did love the transformation.

It felt something like being a giant ball of slime for just a few minutes. She'd grow slippery and then firm up again within minutes with human hands, feet, and a button nose to twinkle at whoever she saw fit. It was a very charmed life Genie Moon lived, and she liked to take advantage of every single second... especially when she got to get away for little bits of time like tonight.

When she was fully transformed, she clicked her night prowl twice. The night prowl, if you didn't know, is the flashlight-like wand that holds all of her radiant, magical light while she takes on another body. It holds it just right and protects it from all harm until she is ready to assume her spot once more in the night sky. So, with the night prowl firmly grasped inside of her hand, she blinked three times and twitched her nose from side to side.

The next moment, she found herself on a wonderfully snow-piled street with crunchy ice cracking beneath her feet. She was dressed in all white— a warm sweater, boots, and a glamorous cross-body sack with rhinestones down the middle and around its buttons. Her makeup was done impeccably just the way she liked it and her night prowl set off her outfit just perfectly as she gazed up and down the street that looked just like it had been plucked right out of a storybook.

This convinced Genie that the writer of "Twas the Night Before Christmas" had been here in this very spot before. It put her in the mind of that poem, hot apple cider, and snuggly, warm clothes all at once.

"It's perfect!" she said out loud to herself, dusting off an old, wooden sign just before her.

As the icy rocks hit the ground, right there, etched into the sign's side were the words she had been waiting to see since she was a little girl. She'd waited so long she could hardly believe that she was reading them now. But she pinched herself and then planted her eyes on the letters one more time. And sure enough, it read the words she'd dreamed of for so many days turned nights:

THE NORTH POLE

Then, all of a sudden, there was a burst of a song right there on the street. Carolers were making their way down the cobble-stoned path that she was standing on. Genie watched them with serious joy etched into her face as they passed her, singing in the most beautiful voices she thought she'd ever heard.

I'll be home for Christmas!
Youuuuu can count on me!
I'll be home for Christmas!
If only in my dreamssssss!

After a few more bars of the song, Genie pinched herself again— only this time, it was to remind herself that she was there with a purpose. She needed to get moving if she was going to get what she came for. She was there to see the infamous

Santa Claus himself. But she knew that it would not be easy to pull it off, especially on Christmas Eve. Still, she knew she had to try. She'd always known that this day would come… that she'd have to ask him for the Mooncharge at some point, so she needed to just brace herself and get in there.

In all of her dreams of making the trip to the North Pole, she'd always envisioned precisely how she was going to do it. Just like Santa did on every single Christmas Eve, she decided long ago that when the time came, she would show up unannounced, slide down his chimney and surprise him with a gift. And that gift just so happened to be over 250 years old. She'd actually waited that long to give it to him on purpose, too. It was the kind of gift that needed a little time to "cook", and she just knew he'd love it.

Most people wouldn't think to come to Santa's home on Christmas Eve. They'd assume that he was off flying around the world, delivering presents. And he was… sort of. But what people didn't know was that Santa was a special being— a very important friend of the skies— so the stars and planets all worked with him to create his very own unique *over*ground tunnel system that allowed him to zip from the North Pole to the skyway and back again within milliseconds. And on these very quick trips, his elves would wait at every chimney to slip Santa the cookies and milk that every family left out just before he zipped in and out of the house at lightning speed.

Genie always thought it was very amusing to watch him pop in and out of chimneys a million times in a row. He was like a big red jumping bean, and it was so much fun to see with her own eyes. Of course, no child could ever catch him red-handed when he was moving that fast. And so his mystery remained. Kids all over the world dreamed of how he did it year after year. And all along, the secret was in his specially brewed lightning potion.

But besides that, there *were* other things about Santa's

trips that no one in the sky could figure out. For example, how did he know who had been naughty and who had been nice? No one could keep tabs on every child, could they? No magic Genie ever saw could do that. And what about the bag? No matter what he delivered to each house, the bag always stayed the same size. And how did he refill it? She knew he took breaks to zip back to the North Pole throughout the night, but that one bag couldn't possibly hold enough presents for the dozens of homes he visited on every trip.

Genie always wondered… what tricks did he have up his sleeve?

But now was not the time to let her mind wander. As she stood in the freezing cold on the highest hill ever recorded in the entire North Pole, she tucked her hands into her pockets where they'd be warm. Then, she began the long walk toward the light that she could just barely see in the distance. Her best assistant, North Anne, (AKA the North Star) had told her that this light was the beacon coming from the highest tower of Santa's Workshop.

That was all she knew, of course, because everything at his headquarters had always been top secret. No one really knew where it was exactly or how it was built. But it didn't matter. This had to be the place. And when she got there, her plan to slide down Santa's chimney would likely take her directly to the house's living room hearth. She could find her way from there, she thought.

But when she arrived at the huge log cabin with the mailbox reading "Claus," she knew her plan wouldn't exactly work the way she'd hoped.

There was no chimney. There wasn't even a roof. In fact, as she stood there staring at the mile-high fortress, covered in gleaming, glistening snow, it was pretty clear that there was no entrance at all besides its very intimidating front door. It was absolutely stunning, but the icicles that were coming down all around the windows and covering the porch were like bars, keeping out anyone that didn't belong. She was still several feet away, but it was very obvious that these were not your ordinary ice drippings. They ran from floor to ceiling on each story of the house. And they were perfectly lined up- the same size and the same shape on every square inch of the extraordinary wooden mansion. And on what would have been the top of the house, all she saw was foggy mist. It was as if the house went up for miles *into* the clouds.

"Gee Whiz!" Genie exclaimed.

This was one of the only places that she'd never seen from up top in her whole life. And, as the moon, there were only a few places that were shielded from her line of sight. That, she knew. It was part of the reason she'd wanted to come down tonight of all nights. And it was the precise reason that she'd picked Santa to ask for help. Of course, there were more magical beings in the universe, but she wanted to also see for herself how this one man captured the hearts of millions of kids all over the world when he only worked one night of the year!

It was absolutely, positively, infuriating to Genie and the Tooth Fairy, Jack Frost, and all the gang that ran Halloween, too. Everyone in charge of granting wishes and making kids smile…. they just couldn't figure out how to be as cool as Santa. It really burned them all up, to be perfectly honest. So she was partly there to find out if he could give her the Mooncharge so that she could help bring the Andrews out of their little pickle… but the other part of her wanted to do a little research.

And so she began her sneaky mission.

Meanwhile, back in San Francisco, things were getting weirder by the minute. Elizabeth was beside herself with worry over the kids, and SisQo was busy calling everyone in town trying to hitch a ride. The only problem was… he didn't know where he wanted to hitch a ride *to*. He had no idea where the kids were and where they'd need to go to find them. According to Cool Greg, one minute, they were fiddling around with the Aerocart's user manual and then, the next second, they disappeared with a zap.

"Like a 'zap' that the TV makes?" SisQo had asked, unbelieving.

Cool Greg had nodded, not knowing how else to describe it or if this was even helping.

"But where would the Aerocart have taken them?" Elizabeth asked on the verge of tears.

"Wherever they would have wanted to go," Greg said, panic in his voice as well. "It would have been completely up to them."

"Great!" said Elizabeth.

And then, she really did begin to cry. She started sobbing so hard into her hands that she could hardly breathe. These were her babies, and now, they were out there somewhere all alone. She felt so helpless. Why had she been arguing and not watching them?

SisQo's heart was breaking as he watched his wife. He stood there numb. His whole body felt like it would collapse. All of the stress and injuries from the entire night started to crash down on him like a ten-ton truck. But what hurt most was the feeling that there was absolutely nothing he could do to help his kids.

"Wait," he heard Juice's voice come from the corner, "Let's be logical about this."

SisQo and Elizabeth looked in his direction.

"I'm listening," SisQo said.

"They're little kids," Juice reminded them. "There's only so many places they'd want to go."

Everyone's expressions started to change as that sank in a little bit.

"You're right." SisQo agreed, "And if I know my kids... they could only be... one of *four* places!"

"The concert," Elizabeth said.

"Home," SisQo helped her.

"Disneyland," they said together, "And the Big Thrill Factory!"

They managed to chuckle a little bit at the fact that they agreed on all of the places their kids loved.

"That leaves two cities to cover," Elizabeth said. "Minneapolis and Los Angeles."

"But... we can't split up," SisQo said matter-of-factly.

"We'll go to Minnesota and check the house and Thrill Factory," Danni said, "You guys go to L.A. They're most likely there trying to make the show."

Juice nodded in agreement.

"But… how are we gonna get there?" Elizabeth asked, "We need to find them soon, and we're hours away from both of those places!"

SisQo turned to Greg and Nick.

"You guys wouldn't happen to have any *more* of your flying golf cart thingies, would you?"

Elizabeth looked uncomfortable again at the thought of actually using one of them, but she waited for their answer. If her kids were flying in one, she could too, she thought. Nick sneaked a look at Greg and smiled back at Elizabeth and SisQo.

"*Do* we?"

"Honey, relax," SisQo told Elizabeth; "We don't have to use the time machine button... we can just fly it, right? Like the sleigh?"

This last question was directed at Greg.

"Absolutely!" Greg replied.

And the next thing they knew, they were following both men down a dark and narrow hallway that led to the back of the giant studio. And when Greg yanked open the big white door in front of them, and they saw what was inside… every one of them gasped in disbelief.

Meanwhile, Genie was actually making progress at the North Pole. She'd figured out that while Santa's home and workshop were guarded by magical icicles (she'd seen a hawk try to rest on one of the window sills and get frozen to the spot immediately), there was exactly one way around this. In the twenty-one minutes that she'd sat outside watching the house, Mrs. Claus had come to the door exactly three times to sit a huge bag outside. What was in those bags, Genie didn't know. What excited her was that she could bet that Mrs. Claus would come to the door again in about 7 minutes (because 7x3 is 21, you see) and when she did, Genie would slip into the house before the door had a chance to shut.

But of course she couldn't go in human form, so she carefully took out her night prowler and zapped herself so that she transformed into a tiny ball of light. And then she waited. And waited.

Finally, after seven minutes exactly, Mrs. Claus opened the door on cue. She set another bag out by the door, and when she did, she was surprised that a gust of wind gathered up at just that very moment. It whipped her skirt all around her and made her lose balance for just a moment as it rushed past. And then, it was gone... just as quickly as it had come.

"Hmmm," said Mrs. Claus, "How odd."

And with that, she walked back inside, closing the door and locking it behind her. Little did she know, Genie was already inside. She'd slipped past the older woman without her even knowing and at the very moment that Mrs. Claus was walking into the kitchen and picking up a cup of hot apple cider, Genie was already making her way up a long, winding, staircase with a huge Christmas tree at the base. The beautiful tree rose through the middle of all the stairs and never stopped for as far up as Genie's eye could see.

She decided that it would be best not to change back into her human form just yet. She would get up to the top faster if she could fly. So she soared up and up and up alongside the tree's gorgeous branches with ornaments sprinkled all throughout its forest green body. She glanced quickly at the rooms on each floor as she passed. There were toy factories and giant candy machines, computers and robots all in neat rows on one level, and even a huge room full of cotton candy on a floor closer to the top.

Then, after several minutes, she was there. She knew she'd arrived because where the floors below had the same kind of wood as the house, this floor was covered in 14K gold... every inch of it. The floors, ceilings, railings and doors... all solid gold. It was simply beautiful.

It was fit for a king... the King of Christmas.

She floated onto the landing to get a better look. Then, she found herself wandering down the hall, looking at all of the pictures on the wall, and admiring all of the Christmas decorations all around. There were beautiful golden wreaths on each door, all in different shapes and sizes. Some were shaped like Christmas trees, and other doors had reindeer, stars, or ornament-shaped wreaths. She wondered what might be behind all of these doors, but she didn't dare check them all. She didn't have a lot of time. She was looking specifically for Santa's office, and she somehow knew that she would recognize it as soon as she saw it.

But then, she got to the very end of the hallway and stopped. There was nothing here but one lone Christmas tree. It was the most beautiful tree that Genie had ever seen. Its leaves were a deep shade of glittery green, with tiny flecks of gold etched into each branch so that it glistened at every angle. And the ornaments were enormous, almost too big for the tree, but they gave it a regal look, almost like one fit for royalty.

Above it was a window where she could see fresh snow falling, and for the first time in a long time, she thought of her childhood Christmases. They'd always been white... with mounds and mounds of vanilla snow. As she stared out, the warmth of the house seemed to envelop her and make her daydream of the days when she hadn't been in charge of granting other people's wishes. There had been a time when she'd made her own wishes, and suddenly, she recalled the joyous feeling of having those wishes come true. She hadn't felt that in a very long time.

Looking a little longer still, she spotted something that looked very familiar. Blowing through the snowy wind, there it was. It was a sky-blue bonnet. And when she squinted to get a better look, she realized that it was... *her* sky-blue bonnet. She'd had it when she was a child. *But how did it get here*, she wondered.

Suddenly, she felt sleepy, and... and... she couldn't think. Why...? What was happening?

"Don't stare too long," a thin, wispy voice floated into her ear suddenly. "That's the Window of Lost Christmases... stare too long, and you'll get lost too!"

The voice was light but snappy. And it pulled her right out of her trance.

"Who's there?!" She cried.

She didn't even know anyone could see her. She hadn't transformed yet, and she didn't know very many people who had the kind of magic to see through her disguises.

"Geronimo's the name," he said warily, "but you can call me Gerry."

"How— how can you see me?"

"I have my ways," he said, a chuckle dancing on the ends of his words.

"Where are you?!" She almost shouted. "Show yourself!"

She looked all around her, down the long hallway, up to the ceiling, behind her. But there was nothing there except her and the Christmas tree.

"Funny that you should tell me to reveal myself when you are the one hidden," he said. "I, myself, am in plain sight."

As he talked, Genie strained her ears, trying to trace his voice to its location. She stopped when she heard it.

But... it was *impossible*.

It seemed to be coming from... the tree! Was this tree alive? She shook her head. That was just out of the question. Even with magic, you couldn't give life to anything that didn't have some sort of energy. And this tree couldn't have energy without roots. This had to be her mind playing tricks on her. Or maybe it was Santa playing tricks on her. Maybe he was somewhere right now watching her and talking to her through an intercom in this tree.

Yes, that's it, she thought.

But just before she dove into the branches to find the hidden intercom, the voice came again.

"For misletoe's sake, I'm *right here!*"

And all of a sudden, she did see something moving. It was so tiny that she should have missed it. Right smack dab in the middle of the tree, on one be-speckled branch, there sat the most prominent ornament of all. And inside, there he was.

Geronimo was the tiniest elf Genie had ever seen. He was a little old man with a thin body and wrinkled face. The glass between he and Genie was thick, but she could see that he was frail. He sat at a tiny little desk, with a tiny phone and small computer. Papers were strewn across the otherwise neat table, and for all intents and purposes, it did look peaceful. The ornament, she saw now, was this tiny elf's office.

"Wow!" Genie exclaimed.

And without thinking, she transformed into her human form right then and there because she just could not resist the urge to touch it.

Lightly, lightly... she brushed the glass with her index finger, wonder filling her eyes. It was so beautiful. And he looked simply enchanting. His eyes were kind and the way he sat there in his bright green suit, his hands folded, and his ears alert made her feel as if she needed to listen to him, despite his size.

"Now that we've been introduced," the elf said curtly, "Please state your business here. I do not believe you had an appointment, Gina Marie Bartholomew."

Genie gasped at the name he'd called her.

"How did you know my name?" She asked, "My *real* name?"

"Santa has records of every living soul on Earth and beyond," Geronimo said simply. "You know that."

And she did. It had just been so long since she'd been reminded of her old life. But she didn't have time for this at the moment. She was Genie Moon now. And she had to see Santa before it was too late for QoQo.

Suddenly, she felt a buzzing in her toes. And that only meant one thing. Someone was making a wish at that precise moment. Genie sighed. She couldn't remember the last time she'd missed a wish. She had to get the Mooncharge, and she had to get it now.

"I need to see Santa," Genie said, standing up straight, "right away."

Geronimo chuckled.

"That's simply not how it works," he said. "Now, if you want to leave a message and..."

"Alright, then you leave me no choice," she said. "I'm really sorry."

And before Geronimo could look up, Genie had reached into her pocket and retrieved a tiny bottle with the words "Crescent Dreams" scrawled across its stained-glass body. Geronimo was still talking as she placed her delicate finger on the spray button.

He never saw it coming. Mid-sentence, she pressed the button, and the light mist covered the entire ornament. And within seconds, he was out like a light. She picked up the ornament gently to bring it to her face. She was looking for some clue for how to find Santa's office on her own when suddenly, she heard a click.

And then... right before her eyes, the wall behind the tree disconnected from the rest of the wood. The window that had been above it shuttered to a close. And the wall swung open to reveal a huge room, covered from floor to ceiling in pure gold. It shined so brightly that it gave the impression of actually glowing from the inside out.

And there it was... the chimney that she'd searched and searched for since she had arrived. It was directly across the room with a giant chair sitting in front of it like someone had been sitting there warming themselves by the fire.

She couldn't waste any more time. This was it. She had to do this for QoQo... for her family. She needed help making the wish come true, and she couldn't do that without the Mooncharge. Santa was the only one that could help, she reminded herself. So she took a deep breath and stepped over the threshold and into the room.

There was a giant clock hanging over the fireplace that was now counting down to something. Looking around at the empty room, she assumed that it was counting down to Santa's return and so she counted her lucky stars that she still had time to prepare.

She had exactly three minutes and twenty-four seconds, so she got to work.

Now, she'd planned everything out to the tee. She knew that there was only one way to appeal to Santa now that she'd broken into his house needing a favor. He would be disappointed in her, maybe even angry, so she knew that she had no choice but to appeal to his *hungry* side.

And she knew something else too-- that she had the tastiest gifts in the whole world. And so the next moment, she was digging in a purse that no one else could see. That's because it was connected to her secret stash up in the heavens. The deeper she dug into the invisible purse, the more her arm disappeared. Minutes later, her arm was so far into the pouch, that it looked like she didn't have an arm at all. She was trying to grab the brownies that she'd baked. She'd added a strong batch of lightning potion into the batter, and they were by far the best she'd ever made.

"If I could just... reach... far... enough...!" she grunted.

But her search was interrupted and her heart nearly stopped when she heard a voice behind her.

"Just what *are* you doing?!"

It was a deep, booming voice coming from the fire. And it did not sound jolly.

All Genie could think was that there was no way that three minutes and twenty-four seconds had gone by that quickly. And her brain was all tied up with fear, so she said the only thing that popped into her head at that moment.

"Well, you're home early."

What Genie wasn't aware of was that SisQo and Elizabeth weren't waiting around for her or Santa Claus to help them. They were taking matters into their own hands. With the help of the Kinda Funny squad, they were seconds away from taking flight to Los Angeles.

SisQo had chosen a very sporty, Ferrari-style Aerocart from their very impressive collection. He and Elizabeth were climbing in when they heard the old version of "I'll Be Home for Christmas" come in on the cart's radio. This used to be Elizabeth's favorite Christmas song. *That is, until tonight,* she thought. And before she knew it, a feeling had crept up inside of her heart. She didn't quite know how to describe it, but it made her entire body slump inside the seat of the cart. But she tried hard to stuff the feeling down. She merely leaned against her husband as they moved slowly through the garage of the Kinda Funny studios.

Greg's instructions had been simple. They were to drive up the winding parking structure until they reached the seventh level. This was the roof, he'd told them. But the key was to gain speed all along the way. And then came the scary part.

"There's a runway when you get to the seventh floor," Greg was explaining again over the cart's video conference system, "Floor it when you get there, and just before you get to the edge, you're going to press the button right there."

Greg pointed upward, and right above the screen that he was talking through, SisQo saw the red button that read, "Flight."

"Yo, are you sure about this," SisQo asked almost unbelieving. "What if that doesn't work?"

"It's going to work," Greg replied simply. "Now, look… it's coming up! You've gotta really step on the gas to get your wings."

SisQo and Elizabeth could see the roof coming into view plain as day. They held their breath as SisQo shifted gears to engage the turbo engine just like Greg had told him earlier. When that was done, he said a quick prayer before pressing his foot harder on the gas. Elizabeth couldn't bring herself to watch this part. She decided that she trusted her husband, so she didn't need to look. *He could handle it,* she thought. And so, just like in the sleigh, she buried her head in his arm and braced herself for whatever was about to come.

It felt like hours when it could have only been seconds, but SisQo focused in like a laser as the edge of the building came into view.

"Press it…NOW!" he heard Greg yell into the camera. "Press the button!"

And after taking the deepest breath he'd ever taken, he lifted his finger up to the button and in one swell motion, he pressed it and closed his eyes. As he felt the ground disappear beneath the cart, he turned and covered Elizabeth's entire body to protect her from whatever impact might be coming up.

They were huddled together like that, with his hands over her head and body, for almost a full minute before they realized that... nothing had happened. Absolutely nothing. SisQo sat up again and looked out of the side of the cart, and all he saw was a huge cloud surrounding them on all sides. It was closing in on them like cotton candy, and it felt kind of like swimming through a million pillows before they broke free and soared up further and further until there were no more clouds... just open, blue sky.

"We made it!" SisQo shouted, pumping his fist in the air with pure joy and relief, "Greg, we made it!!"

On the screen, all of the Kinda Funny guys were doing five different kinds of victory dances. And watching them made SisQo and Elizabeth smile for the first time since the kids had disappeared. Honestly, though, they still didn't know how to feel. They still hadn't heard from QoQo or Ryu, and it was making Elizabeth positively sick with worry.

She couldn't believe that she'd gotten her hopes up and that she'd started to believe... in magic. For a few short hours, Christmas had come alive and the dreams of her childhood... the early days when she'd actually waited up for Santa and made him cookies on Christmas Eve... they'd come back.

No, even better than that... they'd come true.

Her dreams... they'd come true. And then, they were taken away from her again within seconds.

The thoughts bounced around in her brain for several minutes before she felt huge drops of tears coming down her face. She had never cried this much in one night. Honestly, she hadn't known that these feelings were still deep inside of her. She hadn't known that she was still holding out hope that this kind of carefree, innocent joy could all be real. But seeing Genie, riding in her sleigh, and seeing the magic they passed on to all those people in that stadium… it did something to her. It stirred something inside of her.

And now, that was all mixed up with the worry and dread of losing her kids.

She literally didn't know how to feel.

Right at that moment, as if right on cue, the phone that she'd gotten from Greg back at the studio rang in her pocket. And when she took it out and stared down at the caller I.D., she read her stepdaughter's phone number as it flashed across the screen. Shai was SisQo's oldest daughter, and over the years, she'd become like her own too. She couldn't imagine how she'd gotten the number, but looking at the time, she prayed that she was only calling to say 'Merry Christmas.' It was too late for anything else but an emergency, and they just couldn't take any more bad news.

"Hello?" Elizabeth answered, making a face at SisQo. "Shai, is everything OK?"

"Take the phone from your ear," Shai's voice blared over the speaker. "I'm on FaceTime! Greg patched me through."

Elizabeth pulled the phone away from her face and saw that she was right. There, filling the screen, was Shai's very concerned face. She was wearing a red Santa Claus hat and the earrings to match. But her expression looked anything but jolly. Her brow was creased, and her face said that she was more than a little confused.

By now, SisQo had turned the Aerocart onto autopilot and leaned in so that he could talk to her too. He heard the distress in her voice and knew that there was only one thing she could be calling about. They'd just crashed sleigh-first into a football stadium. Then, they'd escaped in a speeding golf cart after angry fans begged for an encore. He knew exactly why his daughter was calling looking for answers.

"We made the news, huh?"

"Um, yeah! Dad, what were you guys doing in that... what was that thing you flew in on, anyway? People are calling it a UFO on Twitter."

"Shai, it's a long story. Your sister"— but he stopped talking when he thought about Ryu and QoQo.

He was so worried about them that he could hardly make the words come out. He hoped that wherever they were that they had what they needed. He hoped that they were warm and that they weren't hungry. Seeing Shai's face had reminded him just how special each one of his kids was to him. He couldn't stand the thought of any of them suffering.

And not only that, he thought, what if QoQo was somewhere blaming herself for all of this? What if the reason she'd left was because she felt like she needed to help him get his talent back? What if this was all his fault? He should've told her that he didn't care about any of that. All he wanted was for them all to be together... for all of them to be safe.

This was his family, and it was his job to protect her... not the other way around. He had to find them, no matter what it took.

"Shai, I have an idea," SisQo said, "and I need your help."

6

QoQo Star Is Coming to Town!

"Come now! You'll listen to reason, won't you?" Genie tried to make her voice sound softer, more soothing.

But it wasn't working.

"You break into my home, flash freeze my assistant, and ruin my last break of the night," Santa bellowed. "And on Christmas Eve, no less! Now, you want me to listen to reason? Out, out, out!"

Genie knew that he'd be upset, but she never thought he would scream at her. Let's be real... no one wants to be yelled at by Santa Claus... not even if you're over 200 years old like Genie. She had to think of something to calm him down. She was having trouble finding the gift she had planned on giving him, so that would have to wait, but there had to be something she could do or say now that would convince Santa to help her.

"Ok, I know you're angry," she said, backing toward the door. "And I'll leave if you want... but please, just hear me out."

Santa didn't move. He just grunted. The red had gone from his apple-like cheeks. And nothing was moving in his entire body except the whiskers on his face. They kept quivering in angry little spurts and she knew that he must be fuming inside. She had to talk fast.

"OK, um... there's a family. The Andrews," Genie started talking as quickly as possible. "I was supposed to help them, but something went terribly wrong. My magic, I-- it started to die right in the middle of QoQo's wish and the sleigh— and the game— "

Before she knew it, Genie had started sobbing right in the middle of her speech. She didn't know how her emotions had gotten the best of her, but there were a lot of things she couldn't explain about this very strange night. Even still, she knew she had to keep going before she was kicked out onto Santa's snowy lawn. He needed to know how much trouble everyone was in. But before she could open her mouth to speak again, Santa's voice rumbled in a low tone.

"I know all about it," he said and turned back toward the fire.

Genie's face went pale. Had she heard him correctly? He knew what had happened?

"But how? This was on my watch. Weren't you delivering presents? How could you know?"

Santa didn't say anything right away. He just nodded his head in the direction of a giant snow globe in the far corner of the room.

"That's my Christmas tracker," he said. "It tells me whenever a family's Christmas is getting off track... that is, if

Christmases are getting ruined."

"You can see all that?" Genie asked in astonishment.

Santa didn't answer. He just kept explaining how the tracker worked.

"First, they were all on track to have the perfect Christmas," he said. "But then, something happened. I rushed to try to see what was going on, but of course, my powers don't allow me to be seen at night, so I had to work from afar."

"Wait, what do you mean? Why can't you be seen at night?" Genie asked carefully.

"How easily you forget, Genie," Santa said. "I got my powers from the sun, remember? And he has great power… solar energy is almost limitless. It only meets its match when it encounters the nighttime— that's *your* territory."

"Yes, I guess you're right," Genie said thoughtfully.

"That's why I watch very carefully when children are awake," he continued. "And you watch them when they're sleeping… or when they're *supposed* to be sleeping. I've always thought that we were a pretty good team, although we don't talk as much as we could."

Genie had never thought of this. They should work together. It made perfect sense. Why hadn't they realized this a long time before?

"Yes," was all she could think to say.

"Of course, I've gotten some clues as to who might be behind the distance between us… and the unfortunate events of tonight."

"Clues? Someone?" Genie looked confused, "You mean, you think someone tried to ruin Christmas Eve... *on purpose*? But who?"

Before Santa could answer, there came a loud noise from the chimney. It sounded like a RATTLE, then a loud CRASH. And then, almost suddenly, they appeared... all *three* of them.

"I knew it!"

"Tilly?" Genie's lips quivered as she spoke. "Peter... Jack?"

The sight of the three people she saw standing in front of her almost made her knees buckle. Tilly, the Tooth Fairy, Peter the Easter Rabbit, and Jack Frost were the last ones she expected to be behind something like this. They were all in this together— the five of them. They were the pioneers of wish-making. They made people happy all over the world. So why were they here, wands and magic swords drawn?

"Oh, don't look so surprised, Genie," Peter Rabbit was saying. "This has been a long time coming. And of course, we picked the best night... all of America is watching as the disaster you created with SisQo's family is on every news channel!"

Of course, Genie thought. *They'd waited for QoQo's wish... they wanted the entire world to see her destroyed.*

That's when she saw Tilly recording on her phone as Peter shot a blast of light in her direction, only missing by a hair. Before Genie could recover, he was shooting off another and another. Genie spotted something that she hadn't recognized before. Peter's eyes... they were the same shade of dark as the man on the football field— the one that had been holding SisQo hostage in the stadium earlier that night. Tilly sprang into action while Genie was distracted, turning her back to Peter and firing off pinwheels at Genie and Santa as they ducked and dodged them all.

"Stick to the plan," Genie heard Jack say icily. "I've told you... this one's mine."

And he slowly approached Genie with a widening grin. Her stomach lurched and she wanted to evaporate slowly, but she could feel that her powers were even weaker than before.

"What's the matter, Genie? Feeling helpless?"

Jack's voice froze Genie from the inside out. He walked closer to her, his eyes burning and his fists clenched into a raging ball of fury.

"I know how you're feeling," said a voice that sounded far away. "Left out of one of the world's most important holidays. But let me tell you something... it's not what it seems."

It was Santa talking.

"We wish we had help. We wish that we could share the holiday with all of you," he continued. "I'm responsible for millions of kids all over the world every Christmas... I haven't spent the holiday with my wife in over 50 years! And let me let you in on a little secret... today is her birthday!"

Jack looked all around him, searching for the words to say. When it was obvious that he had no response to this, Tilly decided that it was her turn to take over.

"Don't be weak! We came here for a reason," she barked at Jack. "We've been slowly draining your powers for the past moon cycle. We almost have it all, so tonight will be your last night as Genie Moon... any last wishes?"

The words stung as they came out. Tilly, Peter, and Jack

had all stepped forward, drawing their wands and swords. Genie couldn't think of a way out, and when she glanced up at Santa, he seemed not even to be trying to think. He was just standing there, watching them come closer.

And as they closed in, she found herself not even thinking about her own life... she wasn't even thinking about the fact that she was about to lose all of her powers. The only thing she could think was that QoQo still hadn't gotten her wish. She was still out there in who knows what kind of danger. And at that moment, she decided that no matter what happened to her, she would not break Lunar Law. A child had come to her with a wish and she would grant it even if it was the last thing she did.

So she closed her eyes and clenched her tiny fists at her sides. Then, she did all she could do to focus her mind on QoQo, envisioning her making it to the concert and making her entire family proud. Genie created a picture of her getting her father's talent back... and returning home overjoyed that Genie had given them the perfect Christmas. Genie figured that if she could just visualize it, maybe it would actually happen. And she tried hard to believe that with all of her heart.

"What is she doing?" Genie heard Tilly ask. "You silly woman, don't you see? We've already won! There's nothing you can do now but surrender the last drops of your powers to complete the transition."

But Genie could feel those last drops gathering into the tips of her fingers. There was a heat rising through her entire body. She felt like she would burst any minute if she kept on like that. But it was a good feeling... a powerful one, so she kept going. She felt Tilly, Peter, and Jack shifting uncomfortably in front of her but she dared not open her eyes. She was almost there. Sweat was forming on her brow and tingles started to make waves through her arms and legs. And then she heard it... or had she only felt it? She wasn't sure. But it happened. It was a small POP that let her know that her magic was activated. And just moments later, white light burst from her body in a blinding flood of glowing power.

Everyone stepped back in amazement.

The light lifted Genie off the ground, and somehow she just knew... she knew she'd done it. QoQo would get her wish. Everything would be ok. She didn't know how or how long it would take, but Genie's legacy would be that she left this world fulfilling her purpose. And so now, she was ready for anything.

She faced Peter, Tilly, and Jack once more and looked them in the eye. She was ready to say that she didn't care what they did to her now. She was ready to say that she surrendered. But she was stopped in her tracks by a hand on her shoulder. Then another.

When she turned to her left side, there was Santa. And when she turned to her right side, there was Mrs. Claus... beaming from ear to ear.

"Why"— Genie stammered. "Why are you smiling?"

"Because you did it!" Mrs. Claus exclaimed, "They can't touch us."

And for the first time since she'd made the decision to will QoQo's wish into reality, she really looked at the people standing before her. They were surrounded by a white light... her light... and it seemed like they were frozen in place.

"Bound in place... by *your* magic," Mrs. Claus said, smiling wide.

Genie couldn't believe it.

"Wait... does that mean...?" She could barely talk.

"You came to me looking for a Mooncharge, but it was inside of you all along," Santa said with a chuckle.

"But I'm glad you did come," added Mrs. Claus. "If you hadn't been here, who knows what they would've done to us!"

Genie smiled at this. This night had been absolutely crazy, but she'd learned so much about herself and love and family. She'd even allowed herself to think about *her* family, who she'd lost long ago. But now their memories were clear in her mind. She couldn't help but smile.

"And you know what else?" Santa smiled. "I've even got a present for you."

He moved to the Christmas tracker that still sat in the corner against the wall. It was a beautiful machine that Genie could tell had been crafted from the finest magic.

"How does it work?" she whispered, coming closer.

"Look...there," Santa said, pointing to a tiny snow globe on the far side of the board.

There was nothing but static-like fog inside at first, but as she looked closer, she saw it. It was her house— the one she'd lived in long ago, before she was ever destined to a life among the stars. And in the picture window, she could just faintly see the flashes of four people inside. The smallest one, she noticed, had a slight limp and moved slow. But there was happiness in her movements nonetheless.

A tear came to her eye. She hadn't remembered those days in so long. She couldn't believe how many emotions were coming up for her. And that's when she realized that her childhood made her who she is today. This was the reason that she had to be there for little girls like QoQo... little boys, men, and women, too.

"Congratulations, Genie," Santa whispered. "No longer is your Christmas lost."

All of this time of not remembering, all of this time of stuffing these memories down... blocking out her life on earth... it was getting to her now. It all came bubbling back at once. All of a sudden, she remembered how she'd wished and wished for someone to be there for her... for someone to look up to. She remembered her parents and how she, herself, had sent wishes and prayers up the skies. And now that she was remembering, all she wanted to do was end this night seeing someone else's wishes come true.

"I have to get to QoQo's performance!" Genie told Santa and Mrs. Claus.

"Of course," the older woman agreed. "According to their tracker, the family is on its way to the show right now!"

"And QoQo? Is she ready?" Genie asked.

Mrs. Claus was looking at the tracker with a peculiar expression.

"Hmmm, that's odd," she said.

"What? What is it?"

"I'm not seeing QoQo with them," Mrs. Claus said, squinting her eyes trying to see.

"Wait... what? I've got to get back to my post and see what's going on," Genie said, starting for the door but stopping abruptly before she left. "Thank you so much... for everything."

"Don't forget this!" Mrs. Claus said, digging into Jack's pocket and bringing out a necklace with a moonstone hanging

TILESHA BROWN & SISQO

from it.

"My powers!" Genie shouted.

And she ran forward to get it, then placed the necklace around her neck. And then she was back at the door.

"Good luck!" Mrs. Claus said. "And wish us some, too! We've got many deliveries to catch up on. We lost a lot of time dealing with these three."

She motioned toward Tilly, Peter, and Jack still frozen in place in the middle of the room. Genie looked at them and then at the giant clock over the fireplace, then back at Mrs. Claus again. Santa's back was to them as he checked his list to see where he'd left off. He didn't notice that the wheels in Genie's head were turning again.

"It's 11:35. You'll never catch up at this point without help," Genie said with a glint in her eye. "If I said I had an idea, would you trust me?"

"Are we lost? Tell me we are *not* lost," Elizabeth was talking to SisQo through clenched teeth. "We're on turbo drive… we should've been there already!"

In front of them, several faces were staring at them on FaceChat. The last few minutes had consisted of SisQo dialing up an entire network of his friends and family on video conference. His idea was for everyone to put their heads together and work to find Ryu and QoQo. It was Kevin, his manager in Atlanta, Shai, his niece Jamera, his best friend Nardy, and social media manager, Rishele in Baltimore. His

* 122 *

sister Ranetta and niece Imani were dialed in from Richmond too… as well as his publicist in Los Angeles, Greg in San Francisco, Elizabeth's mother and brother back in Minneapolis, and his cousins, Jamaal and Lily in New York. They were working like a real emergency team, calling every hospital and police station in their parts of the country.

They were also calling the press and putting out announcements of missing children all over every news channel. SisQo's mother and father were even on the conference call, helping to report everything they were hearing and seeing happen in the media as the search for Ryu and QoQo raged on.

"We've got wall-to-wall coverage," they told the team.

"And son, we're here for you… whatever you need," SisQo's mother, Carolyn told him, "Nothing is impossible with God."

SisQo loved the way his mother was always so optimistic. She believed in God with all of her heart, and she always managed to make him feel better about any situation just by reminding him that he was always protected and watched over.

"Thanks, Mom," he told her.

All of this was making Elizabeth feel a little bit better, but she still just wanted her kids in her arms. She was starting to think that she should just take possession of the steering wheel when her phone began to rattle and buzz on the dashboard in front of her. It was so sudden that her heart nearly burst out of her chest from the surprise. She was so shaken up over being lost that her nerves were on edge.

What a night this was turning out to be.

The call was on its last ring when she finally looked

down to see who was calling. She was hoping that it was someone calling to tell them that they'd found the kids… and that they were safe and sound. But it wasn't. At least she didn't think it was. It was a number she didn't recognize. She was about to say that the call must be for Greg and not for her when she stopped dead in her tracks. The phone might not have displayed the name of the person calling, but it did tell her what *city* the call was coming from.

Elizabeth elbowed SisQo forcefully and gestured for him to look. The phone lit up and shook... and right smack dab in the middle of the screen, there blinked a city that they'd never gotten a call from in their life:

THE NORTH POLE.

They were sure that the phone rang a few extra times than usual because it took them a while to get up the nerve to answer. Could this be a joke? Was this another angle the paparazzi was using to get them to comment on the stadium story? Well, there was only one way to find out. Elizabeth's trembling hand rose slowly as she extended her pointer finger toward the green button on the bottom left of the screen.

She paused just before she pushed it and wondered, just for a moment, what she would do if she heard a jolly, old chuckle on the other end of the line. What would she do if this was the very second she found out that Santa Claus was actually real? She didn't know. But she answered anyway, butterflies fluttering madly inside of her stomach.

But nothing could match the feeling of relief Elizabeth felt when she heard the same velvety voice she'd heard from the sky earlier before they even landed in the mess they were in. She'd never been so happy to hear from anyone in her entire life. She was starting to believe that this woman (or moon) was really magic. And she hoped with all of her heart that she was going to be able to use that magic to get them to her babies quickly.

"Genie!" Elizabeth blurted out, and SisQo looked at her in surprise. "Where are you? We need you!"

"I know," Genie said. "And I'm so sorry that I had to leave you to fend for yourselves, but I have my powers back, thanks to Santa. Now, I can help you. Just listen to me very carefully. I'm gonna tell you how to get to your kids in a hurry!"

Elizabeth and SisQo breathed a giant sigh of relief. This was the most fantastic news they'd heard all night, and they strained their ears to hear her clearly. They didn't want to miss one word of the instructions, which turned out to be even crazier than they imagined. According to Genie, they were to change directions entirely and meet her in an undisclosed location. All she gave them were coordinates and a time to meet, fifteen minutes from this moment.

"But… are you sure we can make it so quickly?" SisQo asked.

"I'm sure," was all that Genie said.

And so they put in the coordinates that Genie had given them and turned the Aerocart onto extreme turbo drive, all the way to the fastest speed possible. They were off in a flash, and the world started to blur around them as they went. But then the strangest thing happened. As they approached their destination minutes later, they saw a giant, glowing cloud in front of them.

"What *is* that?" Elizabeth asked, fear rattling her voice.

"I have no idea," SisQo replied.

"What? What's happening? Dad??!" Shai was screaming into the phone, "Dad?! Elizabeth!??"

"SisQo!?!" came several voices on the video conference

at once.

They'd all been talking just a second ago. They'd all been on this journey with them, but now, there was nothing on SisQo and Elizabeth's end except pitch, black silence.

When SisQo opened his eyes, he found himself in a room he didn't recognize. There were bright lights all around, and he seemed not to be able to feel his face. After all that had happened, he didn't even know how his body was managing to hang in there. When he tried to lift his leg, it felt like Jell-O, and it immediately fell to the floor again. His arms did the same thing, and it felt like there was a fire inside his lungs every time he took a breath.

He didn't have time to feel sorry for himself, though, because just then, the space right before him where there had been sitting a chair with a trench coat draped over its back, the air seemed to open up to reveal a… well, he didn't know what to call it. It was like a tornado. And it made him want to get up and run, despite the pain he was in. But just before he moved to try for an escape, a hand started to come through the whirlwind and then, seconds later, Elizabeth's face and entire body lunged through the vortex and landed in a slump right beside him.

"What the…?" SisQo asked, moving to grab his wife.

Just as she was opening her eyes again, a voice came from behind them all of a sudden.

"Time warp," it said.

Both SisQo and Elizabeth whipped their heads around to see who'd spoken. And they saw an old man with wrinkled clothes pushing a mop and bucket. His eyes were sleepy, and he wore a bebop cap pulled down low on his forehead. They stared at him in amazement. And he stared back for a second.

"Are you— do you— know where we are?" asked SisQo, almost afraid to hear the answer.

"Sure," the old man said, "Shrine Auditorium."

"Shrine Auditorium?" SisQo shot up, wincing in pain, "in Los Angeles?!"

"The one and only!" the man said as cheerily as he could, "And I think they're looking for you to start the show."

He pointed to something behind SisQo, and when he looked, he got a glimpse of a stage and a red curtain through the slightly opened door. But when he turned around to ask the man another question, the old man was gone. SisQo looked at Elizabeth, who shrugged.

"Do you think—?" SisQo asked her.

"The kids!" Elizabeth said, and they both jumped up.

But as soon as they were up and through the door, they found the stage just a few steps away. Panic was written all over SisQo's face. This was his show. The man said they'd been waiting for him, so he needed to tread lightly. He needed to make it out of here so that he could find his daughter without anyone noticing that he was there.

But the universe had other plans. Just when he was making his way down the stairs, a lanky kid that looked like he was about 12 years old came running toward him wearing what looked like an usher's uniform. Relief and anxiety were written all over his face as he almost ran SisQo over.

"O-M-G, SisQo, we've been looking ALL over for you!"

he said frantically, "We saw you on the news! We didn't know if you'd make it!"

"I'm here," SisQo said, distracted.

"Well, we have a full house! Over capacity, actually! But most of them are here to see QoQo," the stagehand continued, straightening SisQo's coat. "Everyone in America has been searching for her, and we found her right backstage with her brother. She was here the whole time. Now, everyone's here to see the little girl who disappeared into thin air! And to find out it was SisQo's daughter? Oh, man"—

He seemed to realize that he was talking too much and stopped all of a sudden.

"I'm sorry," he said. "You're good to go!"

The curtain came up, the lights switched on, and hundreds of thousands of faces turned to face SisQo. The music was starting, and his first verse was coming up fast. Tiny beads of sweat formed on his forehead and for the first time in his entire career, he felt… afraid. He was afraid to perform. All of those people had spent their money, and now, he would have to disappoint them. Genie and QoQo were nowhere to be seen, and he knew that if he opened his mouth, nothing would come out.

The cameras pointed in his direction. The reporters were ready to tell everyone on social media how this show went. No matter where he looked or how he tried to think about it, there was no escaping it. This was the end. He decided to back off stage because he couldn't bear the thought of embarrassing himself. No one would love him anymore if he didn't open his mouth… and he couldn't open his mouth because… because… he couldn't—

As he found himself in a dark corner off to the side of the stage, his thoughts were interrupted because right then…

there she was. She appeared on the upper platform of the stage in an outfit he'd never seen before. It was silver and... what was the word? Glittery? Yes, there was glitter everywhere. On her dress, on her wings... yes, she had glitter wings... and even in her hair, which had been swooped up into the cutest pigtails anyone had ever seen. And QoQo looked just like....

"Like a star!" said a voice from behind him.

He spun around to face a woman glowing brighter than anything he'd seen before. He could tell that she was older, but she had a glimmer in her eye that said that she was still young at heart. Her long silver hair flowed down to her knees, and she smiled a most unusual smile... one that made you feel all warm and fuzzy inside. And when she raised her sleeved arms from her side, he realized that her gown had the same shimmer as QoQo's outfit.

That's when he knew.

"Let me guess... Genie?"

The older woman nodded.

"What gave me away?"

Her words sounded like a soft chuckle, and again, SisQo felt that warm feeling all over his body.

This woman has some serious magic, he thought to himself as he walked toward her, tip-toeing further off stage, hoping that everyone was looking at QoQo instead of looking for him.

"Genie—what do I— I can't sing out there! "

But she was shaking her head and pointing back toward the stage.

"Shhh! Look!"

And when he turned around, he gasped. There QoQo was… alongside Juice and Danni now. And she had a microphone in her hand! Within seconds, he saw exactly what his daughter knew all along. She really was made for this! She was holding the microphone and doing the dance moves to his most famous song. Watching her, he felt himself frozen to the spot where he was standing. He couldn't move. He couldn't speak. It was like he was on a different planet. He couldn't believe his eyes.

But his eyes were the least of his worries. He thought he would have a heart attack when he saw her open up her mouth and actually lean into the microphone when the song's chorus came around again. He didn't know what to expect, but he managed to muster up the exact amount of energy to yell out, "Noooooooo!"

He didn't want her singing this song. Not this one. And what would happen if the crowd didn't like her voice? He had to protect her. He had to—

But he was too late. The volume of the music drowned out his cries and moments later, all he heard was the sound of his baby girl's voice soaring across the auditorium like the open sleigh they'd rode across the country in earlier that night. Would this whole experience crash and burn for QoQo just like that sleigh did? He'd never heard her sing a full song and he couldn't really hear her voice now over the nervous chatter he had going on in his head.

But what he did hear was applause not even a minute later. *Applause?!* He felt so confused. What was happening?

"Let me rewind that so that you can really catch the moment," he heard Genie say.

And he felt the entire world winding up like one of those toys you get at fast food restaurants. He saw the whole scene before him reeling back to the moment just before QoQo opened her mouth. And when everything was going in forward motion again, this is what he heard:

Let me sing my so-o-onnnnnng!

I like it when the beat goes
Duhn-a Duhn-a
Get up, make your hands go...
Duhn-a Duhn-a

Let me sing my so-o-onnnnnng!

The melody was the same, but the words were QoQo's. SisQo looked shocked and overjoyed and completely overwhelmed at the same time. He couldn't believe this was his baby girl on the stage singing in front of all of these people. She sounded amazing. She looked amazing. He was literally at a loss for words, until four... only four words... finally came to mind.

"My QoQo's a star," he whispered to himself.

And at that moment, Genie raised her night prowler and tapped it against the air. Immediately, SisQo felt an ice cold sensation run through his entire body. He felt magic coursing through his bones, snapping something into place inside his soul. And he knew right away... it was back — all of it. He was whole again. His baby had done it! She'd become a star and lifted the spell.

"Could you have asked for a more perfect Christmas?" asked Genie.

She fully expected him to leap for joy, but instead, SisQo just looked down at the floor. Genie's smile faded. She searched his face for clues as to what he could be sad about at a moment like this. He had his talent back, everyone was safe and sound, and he was spending the most wonderful time of the year with his entire family. What more could he want?

But then she stopped.

Of course, she thought.

She knew what it was before he even uttered the words.

"Uh, Genie… I don't want to sound ungrateful because everything is *almost* perfect… but…" SisQo said, looking at the floor, "I just wish Shai was here, too."

Genie looked at him for several seconds. He looked up at her and she saw a flicker of a memory there. It was a memory of Shai at QoQo's age… she'd been a singer too… a star. She'd even been in a music video for the very song that QoQo was singing. Shai had been his first little star, and Genie sensed that the whole night had reminded SisQo of just how much he missed Shai being that age… and just spending time with her in general. Right then, Genie just nodded her understanding. Then, she smiled.

"Well, it's a good thing I'm in the wishing business, huh?"

With just a flick of Genie's wrist, the night prowl produced a huddle of people right before them, backstage. And it was everyone that had been on the video conference call trying to find QoQo that night, plus *more*. Everyone was confused about how they'd gotten there all of a sudden. But there was no time for questions because there was no time for explanations. It was all way too complicated.

Just hug already, Genie thought.

And they did.

"Mom, Dad, Jamera, Imani!" SisQo exclaimed, "You guys are here!"

Just behind them, there was SisQo's sisters, Donisha and Ranetta... his nephew, Little Charles... Elizabeth's brother Chris, his kids Chris Jr., Christian, and Cailee. Even Nardy was there with his wife, Dawn and their kids Brinden, Renise, and Raven. SisQo's mother and father, Elizabeth's mom... everyone was there! The entire backstage area was buzzing with happiness and genuine excitement.

But there was someone still missing.

SisQo searched and searched, but he didn't see her. Of course, Genie was already all over it, though. She grabbed his shoulders and gently turned him in the direction of the stage... and just across the way... waiting in the wings... there she was. She was dressed in a beautiful floor-length, sequined gown. The sequins on the dress glistened in the light, making her glow from head to toe. Her hair was a crown of curls perfectly arranged on her head, and as she emerged from the curtain, she seemed to float onto the stage, holding a microphone. His mother, Carolyn, was behind her and SisQo couldn't help but to get emotional. He loved his family so much.

"Are you OK?" Genie asked SisQo, who was still staring in amazement.

"Yes," he said, wiping a single tear from his eye, "She's just so beautiful. And I can't believe it. She never sings anymore."

"Christmas has a way of bringing things out of you," she said.

*Illustration inspired by photo taken by Rishele Ellison of Shelli Snaps

And then Genie nudged him forward. When he looked up, he noticed for the first time that both of his daughters were now beckoning him toward the stage to join them. Suddenly, the scrawny stage assistant with the glasses hanging off the end of his nose ran to SisQo and helped him into a custom dragon jacket.

SisQo adjusted it to fit and then ran out on stage with his kids. There were three microphones, one with a diamond-crusted dragon attached, another with QoQo's star, and one more with the classic treble note that stood for the music that lived within his first baby girl, Shaione. QoQo and Shai smiled big as he joined them and the band began to play a song that he'd never performed before. He turned to find his Music Director, Nate, smiling at him, knowing that this was the most appropriate song for them to sing at that moment because this had turned out to be a night to remember… it truly *was* a perfect Christmas.

And everyone in the audience seemed to agree as they joined in singing the lyrics.

On a silent night
Reindeer prepared for flight
And Santa's on his way…

It seemed like the whole world stopped for SisQo and his girls at that moment as they sang together in perfect harmony. Shai and QoQo looked absolutely stunning in their gowns. No one could deny that there was pure magic on that stage. And it only magnified when the whole family joined them and started to sing too.

No matter if we buy nice gifts,
Cause I'll scratch everything on the list.
Just as long as I spend it with you,
It's a perfect Christmas!

And as if it were pre-destined, they sang the very last note of the song at exactly 11:59 PM, then took a bow, thinking that it could never get any better than this!

*Illustrated by SisQo

How could it? Elizabeth was crying happy tears and every one of the children were jumping with glee. They'd done it. They'd pulled it off and QoQo, for one, could not be happier.

But little did they know, it wasn't over yet.

* 136 *

Suddenly, as the clock struck 12, the ground began to rumble and the world started to spin. And the next thing they knew, SisQo, Elizabeth, and the kids were inside a sleigh similar to the one they'd first hitched a ride in earlier that night. But this time, they weren't afraid. They weren't even all that surprised. As they rose high above the city, they waved at the huge lamp in the sky lighting their path toward home.

"Thank you, Genie!" Elizabeth called out. "Merry Christmas!"

And they could've sworn that they saw her wink at them as they soared up and over a huge cloud, disappearing toward Minnesota once again.

Elizabeth was cuddled next to SisQo in the first seat of the sleigh as Ryu and QoQo sat in the back with Elizabeth's mom. She couldn't take her eyes off of her daughter. She was so happy that she'd finally started to believe. She'd tried to convince her for years that Genie existed, and now it felt like they all shared something so special, she could hardly stand it. Chris was in a sleigh next to them with his wife.

But the entire rest of the Dragon family trailed behind, taking care of much more important business. They were all in different styles of Aerocarts, with gifts loaded onto the backs, soaring in different directions. Chris, Jr., Christian, Cailee, Jamera, Charles, Imani, Brinden, Renise, Raven, Nardy, and Dawn— even SisQo's publicist and social media manager were all in different carts, blasting from house to house making deliveries for Santa. And ever so faintly, you could see a flash of red light jumping from chimney to chimney after them, making sure to pick up the cookies and milk at every stop.

Genie smiled. She'd saved the Andrews... she'd saved Christmas... and she'd saved herself. Now, all she'd have to do was make it to next year... when she'd most likely have to do it all... over... again.

"I was so scared, Grandma," QoQo looked up at her grandmother. "I didn't know if mom and dad would ever find me. I thought we were going to spend Christmas all by ourselves."

"Yeah, I thought they were leaving us behind…" said Ryu, "…because we'd been naughty and went to the show alone."

"But we only did it so we would make it on time and daddy would get his voice back!"

Their grandmother gave them both a squeeze and shook her head.

"Of course you did. We know that," she said warmly, "And just for the record, you would've never been left behind. Your Christmas guides would have never let it happen!"

"Christmas guides?"

"Of course! Look!"

And just as she pointed to the reigns on the sleigh, there appeared out of nowhere, four blonde-haired reindeer with skin the color of mahogany and antlers that stood about six feet tall. The same twinkles they'd seen earlier were surrounding the beautiful animals from head to toe. And with every shake of their manes, they sent warm quivers down QoQo's spine. One look at them and she knew: this was more magic. But where had they come from? QoQo looked all over the sleigh for clues. She knew they hadn't been there before. So why had her grandmother called them "her guides"?

"Grandma? Those reindeer were *not* there all along, and I know they weren't," she said matter-of-factly.

"Oh, they were there. It was your faith that wasn't there before," her grandmother answered back quickly.

"*My* faith? I believed in Genie more than anybody in my family! I believed in Christmas wishes. I believed the cookie's fortune!"

"You believed in all of those things *because* of the cookie's fortune, didn't you?" her grandmother asked calmly, her voice soothing like hot chocolate, "You believed in all of those things. But you didn't believe in yourself... until now."

And then it dawned on QoQo. Something didn't seem right.

"Grandma, I thought you said that I needed to have faith to even get Genie to appear," QoQo said. "If my faith wasn't there, then...?"

Her grandmother smiled a little at this.

"I may have helped just a little bit," her grandmother said.

"How?"

QoQo sat up straight and turned to look her grandmother in the eye, who immediately saw that her little QoQo had grown up a lot in just the few hours she'd been gone. She was smarter, more mature. Her babies could handle the truth, she thought to herself, and so she proceeded to tell her grandchildren the entire story.

"Let's see... where should I begin?"

The rest of the way home, she told them all about how she had worked with Genie to get things just right. She'd folded a specially-made fortune into the cookie and made sure that

QoQo opened it that first night on Chinese New Year. She'd taught QoQo how to make snow-skinned mooncakes for Genie because she knew they were the moon's favorite. And she was also the one that made the wish to get them out of San Francisco when it seemed that all hope was lost. That was how she knew to have a feast ready for them when they got home... even when the rest of the world thought that QoQo and Ryu would be lost forever.

It turned out that Genie Moon owed Gram a favor for the many years it took for her to teach Genie the Vietnamese language and customs. Before Genie met their grandmother, Genie had never visited any of the Vietnamese children in any of their villages.

"And when our lessons were complete all those years ago," she told them, "We worked together, with those children, to end the Vietnam War."

"What's the Vietnam War?"

"Your grandpa Alonzo knows that story a little better than I do," Gram said, "I was just a helper. He was a fighter."

"Grandpa Alonzo fought in the war?" Ryu asked, surprised.

"He helped to win it," Gram said, smiling.

"Wow!"

"So, you see..." she said, "giving our QoQo a star was the least Genie could do. We're a blessing to each other. God brought us together when we needed each other the most. And that's the reason you kids have all that you ever desired. We have *all* of the heavens looking down upon us."

"It's why we're stars, right Grandma?" QoQo asked.

"And don't you forget it," she said.

And they never, ever did forget... as long as they all lived... which was, of course, happily ever after.

"Grandma?"

"Hmmm?"

"What did you cook for the feast?"

"Oh...just your favorites: Chicken soup, sticky rice, pork buns, roast goose, Christmas pudding..."

"And the best sweet potato pie you ever tasted!" said Carolyn Andrews from the next sleigh.

The kids roared with cheer.

"Yahoo! Merry Christmas!!"

The reindeer jolted higher through the clouds, dipping and soaring through the diamond sky. It was so magical. They were gliding in and out of clouds like they were on the most beautiful rollercoaster in the history of time. QoQo stole a glance at her family, all buckled in and nestled close.

This is what Christmas is all about, she thought.

And according to Genie Moon and all of her glittering stars... QoQo was absolutely right.

The End!

Sneak Peek of...

"CHRISTMAS IN BALTIMORE"

DEDICATION

For Jacqueline and James Owings, who were angels on earth and who now watch over their children from heaven.

EPILOGUE
(A VERY) SILENT NIGHT

'Twas the night before Thanksgiving in a little row house...

Where one little boy lay up, awake on the couch.

He was looking at the fireplace for any sign of life...

For all year long, he'd been nothing but nice.

And his one wish to Santa was for him to come early...

He was to come right at midnight... and it was now 11:30.

Tick tick... tick tock... the little clock said.

As he listened real close... making sure mom stayed in bed.

Now, you may wonder why he called Santa early this year...

Well, there was something very special happening for Tamir.

He'd dreamed a big dream and he knew it was the one.

He knew it could change his life for many years to come.

He was hoping, wishing, praying... for a phone call this night.

One that would take him out of harm's way and into the spotlight.

The call was for a record deal- his every wish come true.

He'd auditioned and they said, "We'll get back to you."

That's when he got the idea... he'd call on Santa to be safe.

He needed magic, he reasoned, he couldn't leave this up to fate.

This was all he wanted for Christmas... no toys under the tree.

Just for his mother to stop worrying... and leave Baltimore in one piece.

If it happened, he promised he'd come back and help one day.

If only Santa came through... and that phone call came today.

But in order for it to work, and Santa knew it too...

His star would need more time to rise before his wish came true.

As soon as the clock struck 12 that night, in that moment, Tamir knew.

Santa wasn't coming, not that day, or any time soon.

If he wanted to be a star, he thought, he'd have to do it himself.

One day his name would shine in lights- he didn't need anyone's help.

Right then, it was decided... and as he grew into a man...

He vowed to never believe in Santa ever again.

"Be careful," his angels warned in a dream that very night.

"You never rush a star," they said, "No, never one this bright."

For, he couldn't understand it then, but a few years down the line,

He'd finally get his wish... one starry Baltimore night.

ABOUT THE AUTHOR

Tilesha Brown is a writer, publicist, and publisher from
Los Angeles, CA. Her whole life, she has wanted to
change the world by transforming blank pages into magic.
She created the SAUCEBERRIe universe for children and
adults who struggle with believing in the magic that exists
in the world... and inside themselves. Through Genie
Moon and all of the different people that she meets,
Tilesha hopes that every one of her readers will gain
hope, inspiration, and a will to always keep dreaming!

ABOUT THE AUTHOR

SisQo is a Grammy Award-Nominated recording artist, writer, and CEO of Dragon Music Group— a multimedia entity organized to foster the advancement of music, books, film, and gaming content. Though *SisQo's Perfect Christmas* is his first literary endeavor, he has an array of story-based projects in the works, slated for release in 2019 and beyond. He has always wanted to make a difference through every facet of his artistry— and the literary world is providing a platform to do that... and more!

32680814R00084

Made in the USA
San Bernardino, CA
16 April 2019